HER FAITHFUL COWBOY

A BUTTARS BROTHERS NOVEL, STEEPLE RIDGE ROMANCE BOOK 3

LIZ ISAACSON

ISBN-13: 978-1-63876-138-9

"But he was wounded for our transgressions, he was bruised for our iniquities: the chastisement of our peace was upon him; and with his stripes we are healed."

Isaiah 53:5

CHAPTER
ONE

With only a few days until Christmas, Bonnie Sherman picked her way among the snow in the cemetery to her son's grave. It had snowed a couple of days ago, and the weak December sunlight hadn't made much of a dent in the precipitation. More fog and snow was predicted this holiday season, much to the delight of all who wanted a white Christmas.

Bonnie arrived at the headstone bearing her son's name. Only four when he passed, Jeff would've been rooting for the magic of snow on Christmas Eve. The thought brought a haunted smile to Bonnie's face. She ran her fingers across the top of the stone, the chill of it radiating deep inside her soul.

She couldn't remember the last time she felt warm. Probably that summer day she'd taken Jeff to the sports complex to fly the kite her mother had given him for his birthday.

Two minutes.

She'd lost sight of him for two minutes.

The next time she saw him, he was dead.

She inhaled, the emotion she usually kept tucked away roaring to the surface. She had good days, and she had bad. Sometimes she'd be going along, busying herself in the third grade classroom where she worked as a teacher's aide, and something would hit her that would release the floodgate on her feelings.

A smell. A random thought. A smile of a student passing by with reddish blonde hair like her son.

She tucked her own strawberry blonde hair behind her ear, wishing she'd worn a hat. Jeff's grave sat in the far south corner of the cemetery, and she laid the denim blanket she'd brought on the ground so she could sit awhile.

She didn't cry, a feat Bonnie had been working on for seemingly ever. It had been five years since Jeff's death, and she thought time should've done a little more healing by now. She started reciting the things she could be grateful for in her life, a strategy her mother had suggested when Bonnie's husband had filed for divorce and left for Maine.

"I have a good job," she said to the silence in the cemetery. Maybe to Jeff. She wasn't sure. She normally didn't talk to him specifically when she came here. She didn't believe he was there, listening.

"I like my job," she continued. "I know some people have good jobs they don't like. But I like working with the kids at the elementary school. They're good kids."

The wind tried to steal her scarf and get its icy tendrils down the collar of her coat, but she pulled the fabric against her skin.

"I have friends. In fact, they're expecting me tonight for dinner and a gift exchange." Her lips curved the slightest bit as she thought about her forthcoming evening of fun, and food, and Christmas spirit.

"My parents have a Christmas Eve dinner planned too." Bonnie didn't hate her life. A life that had been reduced to a few evenings out each month with her friends and remaining family. Most days, Bonnie didn't mind. Some days, she did.

She honestly didn't know how she felt that day.

Sometimes Bonnie simply felt nothing at all, and as the wind whipped up the top layer of dusty snow and attempted to throw it in her face, she couldn't work out how she felt. So it was one of those days.

"Well, my boyfriend is waiting." She smiled at Jeff's name on the headstone and hesitated before standing.

A terrible crash sounded behind her and she turned to see what had caused it. A horse the color of midnight thundered toward her, his head down, his eyes clearly unfocused. She tried to stand, but couldn't, the blanket tangling around her legs.

Snow pushed up her pant leg and all she could see was white—with a huge horse barreling down on her.

"Ho!"

She heard a deep voice echoing in the sky, almost splitting it.

"Over here!" someone else called.

Someone whistled, and Bonnie blinked, trying to get herself to ignore the wild look in the horse's eyes.

"Come on, Bonnie," a man said, latching onto her arms and pulling her out of the way. Pain shot through her body; her heart crashed against her ribs; Fingers and hands like iron kept her moving though her legs acted as dead weight.

She landed in the snow on her back a few gravesites away just as the black horse trampled the blanket beneath his hooves.

She breathed. Her lungs worked.

The whistling started again. Men continued to yell to each other and at the horse.

Bonnie looked up into the most handsome face she'd ever seen. It almost hurt to look at, and she recognized the man immediately.

"Sam." She tried to sit up, but he helped her anyway, the pressure of his hand on her back practically burning through the layers of her coat and clothes.

Sam Buttars. Of course it had to be Sam Buttars with the beautiful face, the strong hands, who'd rescued her. The one man who had caught Bonnie's interest. They'd gone out a few times last summer and into the fall, and then he'd just…disappeared.

He stood and brushed slushy snow from his jeans and offered her his hand. She took it, trying to coach her body to contain the tremor threatening to explode across her shoulders. It didn't work, and her skin tingled where it touched his.

"Hullo, Bonnie." He didn't release her hand but

squeezed it. His intoxicating brown eyes captured hers and she couldn't look away. "Sorry about Thunder Mountain. He's a real pain."

Bonnie couldn't make her voice work, which was absolutely ridiculous. She was thirty-four-years-old, had been married before, had a child, had endured a funeral and a divorce. And yet the simple sight and touch of Sam Buttars stole her breath and rendered her mute.

"Hey, you okay?" His cowboy boots shuffled him a little closer to her and he leaned down to peer at her.

She wished he wouldn't. Because now she could smell him, and though he'd clearly been working all day, the delicious scent of birch trees, leather, and horses accelerated her pulse.

"I'm fine," she managed to say though her legs trembled. "I'm—I just haven't eaten in a while."

Sam finally dropped her hand and fell back a couple of steps. He ducked his head so the brim of his cowboy hat hid his expression. She hated that about him. He'd done it whenever they were talking about something he didn't want to discuss any longer—like why he thought they couldn't have a relationship.

He'd tried to explain, got frustrated, and that was that. Cowboy hat down. Conversation over.

"I need to go help my brothers get that horse," Sam said.

"Yeah, of course." Bonnie moved to retrieve her blanket and brushed the snow and frozen dirt from it. She let her gaze linger on her son's name for a couple of extra seconds before turning to go.

Sam still stood there, and she paused.

"Bonnie," he said, and she wanted to hear him say her name every day. Soft and full of emotion, like the way he just had. In a normal tone, as he called up the stairs so he could ask her a question. In a panic, when he needed her help because the dog was muddy or the kitchen pipes had burst.

"Better go get your horse," she said. "It was good to see you, Sam." She forced her feet to move her further from him.

"What are you doing tonight?" he called after her.

She froze and turned around. "What?"

"Maybe we could go to dinner or something."

CHAPTER
TWO

Sam Buttars couldn't believe he'd just asked Bonnie Sherman to go to dinner with him.

Or something.

The way she blinked at him like he'd spoken Japanese showed that she couldn't believe it either. Her fingers flitted around her throat, and Sam fantasized about kissing her against the pulse in her neck.

Stop it, he told himself. *Stop it now. And apologize. Walk away.*

His brain sent so many short commands, he couldn't sort them all. Couldn't do anything. The four dates he'd gone on with Bonnie a few months ago had been the best ones he'd been on in years. She was definitely the most interesting, prettiest woman he'd had the pleasure of meeting in Island Park.

Island Park. That was the whole problem. He wasn't going to be in town for very much longer, the reason he'd ended things with her in the first place. *Ended* wasn't really the right word. *Ignored* worked better.

So what was with *Maybe we could go to dinner?*

He cleared his throat, the yells of his brothers in the distance urging him to hurry up and join them. It would take all of them to get Thunder Mountain contained again, the brute.

"I can't go to dinner tonight," Bonnie finally said.

"Oh, of course." He stepped backward, his exit absolutely necessary now. "Merry Christmas."

"But I can tomorrow night."

A smile sprang to his face before he could figure out what the heck was going on. It wasn't like his situation had changed. "I just want to explain some things," he said. "I feel bad I never did."

As Sam spoke, he realized he needed closure. If he had to share a meal with beautiful Bonnie Sherman to make sure everything between them was okay, he'd do it.

"I don't have to work for a couple of weeks," she said. "Would lunch work better for you?"

"Whatever works for you."

She tilted her head slightly, swallowed, and said, "Dinner works best for me."

"Dinner then," he said. "I'll come get you around six?"

"Six then." Bonnie gave him one of her shy smiles, the kind she allowed to slip across her face as a mask. It concealed a whole range of emotions he knew teemed just below the surface. Though he'd only been out with her a few times, he'd catalogued her types of smiles, and this one meant she was glad she wouldn't have to spend tomorrow night alone.

She walked away and left Sam standing next to her son's grave. He'd never come with her to visit the site, but she'd told him about it. He looked at it now, with the snow and dirt around it in complete disarray from Thunder Mountain's hooves.

Sam bent and brushed the debris from the headstone, cleared the mulch from the surrounding cement. Jeffrey Jones Sherman. He'd died when he was only four, and Bonnie had told Sam the whole horrific story on their third date.

He'd hated the haunted look in her eyes and the ghostly sound of her voice. But afterward, she'd come alive again, and Sam adored the soft light in her eyes when she spoke of happier things. He'd caught her drifting between her normal self and the shell of herself several times since then, seemingly at random times.

He walked away from the grave and right out of the cemetery, his cowboy boots slipping in the snow. He understood better than most what it was like to be going along, right as rain, doing work he loved, and then running full-speed into a brick wall of sadness. He thought of his parents—his sweet mom who'd taught piano and his hardworking and faithful father who'd worked the Wyoming land—and the less-alive version of himself crept forward.

He caught up to Logan, Ben, and Darren, who had Thunder Mountain tethered to a tree with a single rope. Ben's it looked like.

"He's chewin' right through that," Sam said.

"I lost my rope somewhere." Darren turned in a circle like he'd simply dropped the rope nearby.

"I'm afraid I'll miss," Logan said.

"Give your rope to Ben," Sam said, as the youngest of them all could hit any target, moving or still. Sam released his own rope from his waist and started swinging it above his head. He went round once, twice, three times, and launched the rope toward the giant black head.

He hit his mark and pulled the rope tight, taking his end quickly around another tree trunk. Ben used Logan's rope to add another line to Thunder Mountain, and Darren approached the horse with slow, measured steps.

"You got 'im," Sam said in whispered encouragement. He'd given this challenging horse to Darren to see if his brother could handle it. He'd been doing all right, actually. Thunder Mountain just liked to run free, and he wasn't shy about making sure everyone knew it. Darren would break him soon enough, and then Sam could stop carrying a rope with him everywhere he went.

Ben positioned himself next to Sam for the walk back to Steeple Ridge. "You talk to Bonnie Sherman?"

Sam gave his brother a glare, but he didn't put much malice behind it. Out of the four brothers, only Ben had managed to maintain a relationship of any kind. That had to mean he knew a little bit of how to date and keep a woman happy, right?

A sigh escaped Sam's mouth. "Yeah, I talked to her." He slowed his steps so Darren and Logan, both of whom kept a tight grip on their lines, could get farther ahead. "I'm bein' kind of stupid with her."

"What does that mean?"

"I asked her to go to dinner with me." Sam hated the darkness in his voice. Hated the embarrassment clawing its way through his stomach. "Why did I do that?"

"You like her," Ben said.

Sam had never denied liking Bonnie. Everyone in Island Park knew that. "I'm moving to Wyoming in five months."

"Yeah, that was the reason you used for breaking up with her last fall too."

"It's a good reason," Sam said, glad Ben had stopped calling it an excuse. "Bonnie's never gonna leave Island Park." An image of her son's grave blipped through his mind.

Ben didn't say anything, which only made Sam's skin scratchier. "What should I do?" he asked his younger brother.

His voice must have carried enough desperation, because Ben paused and looked Sam right in the eyes. "A lot can happen in five months. Look at me and Rae. Met, dated, fell in love, all in *under* five months."

A pinch started in Sam's chest. The thought of falling in love that fast made him want to head for the hills. Right now. Not in May. He swallowed, thinking he should call Bonnie, apologize for asking her out, and then cancel.

Ben started walking again, so Sam went with him. "We set a date, by the way. Rae and I. She just booked the church for September fifth."

"September fifth," Sam repeated, but his mind lingered far from Ben and Rae's forthcoming nuptials.

CHAPTER
THREE

By ten o'clock the following morning, Bonnie had cleaned her house from top to bottom and left to right. Since she lived alone, and only had herself to clean up after, it certainly didn't take long to make sure her house smelled like bleach and lemons.

By noon, she'd gone to the gym and showered. She took extra time curling her hair, as Sam had said on their final date that he really liked it curled. She'd thought things between them had indicated there would be a fifth date. And a sixth. And so many that she'd lose count until he finally asked her to marry him.

Looking back, she realized how foolish she'd been. She hadn't said anything to him, but men had a way of sensing a serious woman.

She wrapped another piece of hair around the curling iron, her thoughts drifting to and fro. For the past few months, they always landed on Sam eventually, and they did this time too. They'd never kissed—at least outside of Bonnie's mind. Could she kiss him tonight? What would he do if she did?

He'd said he just wanted to explain some things. For a few weeks after he'd gone silent on her, she'd craved his explanations. Now, though, she wasn't sure she wanted them. She didn't want to hear why he didn't like her, or why he thought they couldn't be together.

She already knew the man was moving to Wyoming. He hadn't kept it a secret, and nothing stayed unknown in Island Park for long anyway. Especially not in a building with ninety-nine percent female teachers.

By one, Bonnie had forced herself to eat an apple and was pacing from the front door to the back. Boyfriend, her, black, gray, and white mastiff watched her from his kingly position on the couch. She ruffled his head on every pass until he finally laid down and looked up at her with a doleful expression.

"Yeah, I know." She flopped next to him on the couch. "I'm being silly."

And she still had five hours to go. She should've said she wanted to go to lunch, but her evenings were definitely her most lonely time. She could fill the daylight hours with cleaning and walking Boyfriend and visiting with her friends. But by evening, everyone seemed to have someone else to see or something else to do.

Night dragged on, the five hours of darkness until she could go to bed almost unbearable. She definitely wanted to go to dinner.

Her phone rang just after three, but she ignored it. She

didn't want to give Sam a chance to cancel on her. She didn't think he simply wouldn't show up if he couldn't get a hold of her. He was too much of a cowboy gentleman for that, and Bonnie too much of a coward to accept he didn't really want to see her.

I just want to explain some things.

Bonnie hadn't had to use much bravery the past few years. It seemed like the Lord knew she'd used all she had to endure a funeral and then weather a divorce. Most of the time she felt like a shadow of herself. A whisper of who she used to be. A shell barely holding a soul.

She pressed her eyes closed and asked for help to know what to do about Sam. Her only feeling was to be brave and check her phone.

So she got up and collected it from the kitchen counter, flipping it over to see who'd called. Cheryl.

An exhale of relief leaked from her body, and she returned her friend's call. Cheryl taught second grade and shared Bonnie's love of fruit smoothies for breakfast. They became fast friends as they waited in line at The Juice Bar before work. Cheryl got the strawberry-mango-banana every day, while Bonnie opted for triple berry with a shot of pineapple juice.

"Hey," Bonnie said when Cheryl answered.

"Just calling to wish you luck tonight." She wore a smile in her voice, and Bonnie remembered her gleeful expression from last night, when she'd told everyone at their Christmas festivities about the confusing dinner invitation from Sam Buttars.

"You know why I didn't answer, right?" Bonnie asked.

"Of course," Cheryl said. "You didn't want to answer in case he cancelled."

Bonnie returned to Boyfriend on the couch. "Maybe *I* should cancel. Put myself out of my misery."

"Maybe you should kiss him like Taryn suggested."

"Taryn's married, so she can say things like that."

Cheryl laughed, and Bonnie envied her friend's carefree nature, the easiness of the burdens she carried. She sobered and said, "Don't cancel, Bonnie. And kiss him when he shows up."

"I'll call you later," Bonnie said, though she didn't really want to re-live the date only moments after finishing it. She'd done that with the first few dates, but this time felt different. Different, because she knew Sam didn't really want to go out with her.

He just wanted to explain.

Bonnie hung up and set her phone on the nearby end table. Boyfriend lifted his face and rested it in her lap. She automatically stroked his head and ears, wondering when her simple life had gotten so complicated.

Six o'clock found Bonnie still on the couch, Boyfriend's jowls still on her leg. Sam came all the way to the door and knocked, causing Bonnie to leap to her feet, her heart palpitating in her chest.

She ran her fingers through her hair, which had flattened considerably from her long afternoon nap on the couch. Boyfriend trotted over to the door, and Bonnie shoved him back with her foot. "No, Boyfriend," she said. "You go to the hall." She pointed behind her, where she'd trained the dog to wait while she answered the door. "Hall. Go."

The mastiff reluctantly went, and Bonnie smoothed her palms down her stomach in anticipation of opening the door.

She expected to see Sam in all his black cowboy hat glory on the other side, and he didn't disappoint. He wore crisp blue jeans and a black leather jacket too. Bonnie's pulse kicked up a notch. In her eyes, the only way Sam could be improved was if he rode a motorcycle instead of a horse sometimes. She licked her lips and said, "Hello, Sam."

He kept both his hands in his jacket pockets as he leaned forward and said, "Hullo, Bonnie." He swept his lips across her cheek and drew back, a flush entering his face. "I don't know what that was."

Her skin throbbed like it had a pulse of its own. "You want to come in?" She stepped back but kept one hand on the open door to steady herself.

He glanced past her. "I thought I heard you say…." He shook his head. "Never mind." Sam stepped up into her house, filling the doorframe with his broad shoulders and commanding presence.

Bonnie tightened her grip on the door as the chill of winter continued to spill into the house, stealing the warmth. She'd never invited Sam inside before. She wasn't sure why she was doing so now.

"Where do you want to go?" Sam asked in a near-growl. He didn't glance around, and Boyfriend didn't come to investigate. Bonnie wasn't sure which unsettled her more. Her dog was usually very protective of her, settling at the corner of the hall until she opened the door, whereupon he'd bound over and sniff and bark at whoever had dared come to bother them.

Sam definitely had a way with animals, something she'd always known but had never truly witnessed.

"How about just coffee?" she asked. The thought of physically eating anything made her stomach tight.

"And doughnuts?" he suggested, and warmth filled Bonnie that he'd seemed to enjoy their first date as much as she had. Even then, the warning signs of his hesitance had been neon and loud. It had taken him a long time to call her again, and even longer to actually set a time to get together.

She wasn't sure she could handle the high influx of sugar—and stay sane in Sam's presence. But she lifted one shoulder and turned toward her coat closet. "Sure. Hopefully they'll have some bear claws."

"I have a hankerin' for a maple twist."

Bonnie couldn't help the small smile that slipped across her face. She'd never seen someone eat as much as Sam could. Not even her ex-husband could pack in so many carbs and go galloping off on his horse without an issue.

He helped her shrug into her coat, and she ignored the zing that shot down her arms and settled in the soles of her feet. Sam put his hand in the crook of her elbow as they moved down the sidewalk, saying, "It's a bit slick tonight."

"The rain's been freezing," she said just to have something to contribute to the conversation. But she felt foolish. Two middle-aged adults should have more to talk about than the weather.

Sam helped her into the cab of the truck he shared with his brothers, which held all the heat of a tropical island. She sank back into the seat as he walked around the front of the truck, her mind churning. Should she stay by the window? Slide over and sit by Sam?

In the end, she wanted to sit by him. She wanted him in her life. So she gave herself an early Christmas present and slid across the seat as he climbed into the truck. The weight of his gaze settled on the side of her face, and she turned toward him.

She employed her bravery. Said, "I like you, Sam." Stretched up and skated her lips along his cheek. Noticed when he leaned into her, a sigh slipping from his mouth.

Satisfied, she folded her hands in her lap and faced the windshield. Her blood moved with the speed of river rapids as he remained still and silent.

"Are we going to get doughnuts?" she asked.

"No." He flipped the truck into reverse and backed carefully out of her driveway. He drove toward downtown, and Bonnie let him have his time to think. Her ex often needed a few extra seconds before he spoke.

Sam needed minutes. Sometimes days. He was utterly maddening, and yet Bonnie was happier sitting in his truck in silence than in her house by herself. She wondered if she'd be just as satisfied with anyone beside her, but quickly dismissed the thought. She knew the reason this inexplicable joy was pumping through her system came specifically from Sam.

He pulled into the public parking lot near the bakery, but didn't get out of the truck.

"Sam?"

"I like you too, Bonnie."

She swallowed, unsure of how to catalog what she was feeling.

His fingers covered hers and then twined between them. "I meant to come here and apologize for my terrible behavior last fall." Sam kept his head ducked and his voice barely louder than the air blowing from the heat vents. "I shouldn't have just disappeared on you. I was making some hard decisions, and you got caught in the crossfire."

"All right, Sam."

"I'm moving to Wyoming at the end of May."

"And that's why you don't want to see me anymore."

"Yes."

"Probably shouldn't hold my hand then." She pulled hers away, shifted to put distance between them though everything in her screamed at her to *move closer! Closer!*

She swallowed, her next words catching in her throat. She forced them out anyway. "I'd like to go home, please."

"Bonnie," he said in a sad, reproving tone.

"This is too hard," she admitted. "I like you, Sam, and you just said you like me too. But we can't be together? Can't even just date for a few months? Can't hold hands and—" Her voice caught. "I want to kiss you so badly." Her throat ached and her tongue felt so dry.

She drew in a shuddering breath, praying for strength. "Please take me home."

"Bonnie."

"Sam." Her voice grew stronger. "Take me home now."

CHAPTER
FOUR

Frustration coiled inside Sam. And anger. And absolute shame.

"I'm sorry," he said after he'd pulled into Bonnie's driveway. She didn't respond as she slid across the seat and got out of the truck. She slammed the door behind her and strode toward her front door with a steady step and strong shoulders.

"You're an idiot," he told himself as he watched her disappear inside her house. He had no right to treat her like this. String her along. Ignore her. Disappear for months. Ask her out again. Kiss her when he came to pick her up.

Seriously, what was that? he wondered as he backed out of her driveway for the second time in twenty minutes. He hadn't been thinking, just doing what came to mind. He wanted to taste Bonnie, so he had. Wanted to hold her hand.

I want to kiss you so badly.

He wanted to kiss her too. He'd enjoyed their time together last fall. Found her attractive physically, emotionally, and spiritually. He loved seeing her at church every week, the evidence of her faith such an example to him.

Sam prayed the entire way back to Steeple Ridge. *Why can't I see what happens? Five months is a long time, Lord. Is it long enough? Have I already ruined any chance Bonnie and I might've had?*

Helplessness rose up and almost choked him. He couldn't swallow as he pulled into the farmhouse driveway.

He sat in the idling truck, sure his brothers knew he'd returned only an hour after he'd left. He didn't want to go inside and face them, but he didn't have to. Ben stepped onto the porch without a coat, folded his arms, and leaned against the pillar.

Drawing a deep breath, Sam got out of the truck. "There's something wrong with me," he declared as he moved toward his brother.

"What did you do?"

Sam sank onto the top step and waited while Ben sat next to him. "First off, I get there and I kiss her." Sam shook his head. "So stupid. So, *so* stupid."

"Like, kiss her on the lips?"

"I wish." Sam scoffed, a crazy idea growing in his head. A crazy idea of jumping in the truck and going back to Bonnie's. Beating on her door until she answered and then taking her in his arms and kissing her. Oh, how he wanted to do that.

"Maybe I should stop fighting how I'm feeling," he said.

"You definitely need to get out of your own way."

"What about—?"

"What about what?" Ben interrupted. "What about you don't overthink everything? What about that?"

Sam stared at the snow in the front yard, which shone a dull gray under the light of the rising moon. He did overthink things. He couldn't help it. For the past ten and a half years, he'd been in charge of keeping the brothers together. And it hadn't been easy, ever.

Farms and ranches rarely needed four men at the same time, one of whom was barely old enough to work. But Sam absolutely would not allow his brothers to split up. Deep down inside him, he'd felt that if he let Logan and Darren go off on their own, he'd never see them again. And Ben? Ben was completely lost for years, dependent on Sam for everything until very recently.

He was used to sleepless nights and long hours on his knees, pleading with God to know what to do and where to go and how to keep the family together. His needs had often come fourth, and Sam had always been okay with that.

That same gut feeling existed inside him now. It urged him to go back to the farm at Coral Canyon and make it successful the way his father had. He knew without a doubt he needed to do that.

It seemed entirely unfair that Bonnie had come into his life at the same time. He glanced over and realized Ben had gone inside.

"Is this some kind of sick joke?" He tilted his head back and looked into the flat, navy sky. Starless because of the storm clouds still hovering over Island Park. "Why lead me to a woman like Bonnie—a woman who'll never leave Vermont—right when I'm ready to leave Vermont?"

God didn't answer, and Sam ended up going inside the farmhouse to continue his prayers so he wouldn't freeze to death right there on the front porch.

———

OVER THE NEXT COUPLE OF DAYS, HE RESISTED THE URGE TO call Bonnie, or text Bonnie, or head straight to Bonnie's house every morning.

Christmas dawned with a cloud-covered sky and a wisp of fresh snow on top of the several inches already on the ground. Sam went out to give the horses their holiday breakfast, Ben only a few minutes behind him.

When they returned to the farmhouse, Darren had fried egg sandwiches on the griddle and Logan was putting presents at each man's place on the table.

"Merry Christmas, boys," Sam said. He washed his hands and waited for Ben to do the same. "Let's do family prayer before we eat, all right?"

None of his brothers argued. They never had. Sam had left home before his parents died, and while he'd loved his brothers, he'd never felt super-close to them growing up. Logan and Darren had that twin bond, often leaving Sam and Ben to each other. Their age difference had been a wide gap as kids, but Sam didn't feel any of that now.

Their parents' deaths had brought them together in ways Sam hadn't known existed. Such a keen sense of gratitude and love for Darren, Logan, and Ben swelled within him that his voice held thick emotion when he asked Ben to say the prayer.

Ben had a way with expressing his thoughts to God, and Sam wasn't the only brother sniffling through the prayer. Ben asked for comfort in this season. He asked for a blessing on the food, on each brother for good health, on his fiancé Rae. Then he said, "Please help Sam as he figures out what to do with Bonnie Sherman."

A healthy pause followed where Sam didn't dare breathe. Surely God wouldn't deny Ben's pure desires.

"Please let Sam put himself first for once." Ben's voice cracked, and tears sprang to Sam's eyes. The prayer ended soon after that, and Sam swiped at the evidence of his emotion. Didn't matter. His brothers were a little teary as they stood too, and Sam wrapped them in a family hug.

Nobody said anything. No one needed to.

Darren finally cleared his throat and said, "Eggs are gettin' cold." That spurred everyone into motion. Sandwiches got eaten, and presents opened, and laughter filled the little farmhouse at Steeple Ridge.

Sitting at the table while Logan chuckled and filled out a Mad Lib, Sam never wanted to leave Steeple Ridge Farm.

———

THE CHURCH DOORS BORE A MASSIVE PINE WREATH AND people streamed through the wind and inside the building.

"We'll probably lose our regular seats," Sam said.

"Probably," Ben agreed.

They increased their pace simultaneously, and sure enough, the chapel was nearly full already. The brothers attended church every week, but dozens of others obviously only came on Christmas.

Ben pointed toward Rae, who held one hand above her head. "I think she saved seats."

Sam followed Darren and Ben down the aisle to a row very close to the front. He hated sitting in the front at church. He preferred to be near the back, on the side, so he didn't have to endure the stares of people he wished would mind their own business.

The people in Island Park hadn't quite treated the Buttars brothers the way others had, though. Sam would admit that the town here had a special spirit about it. A very accepting spirit. No one seemed too worked up that the brothers were orphans. No one brought meals for no reason or patted their arms with sad looks.

Sam was grateful for that. It would be easier leaving his brothers here knowing that Tucker and Missy were here and that the townspeople genuinely seemed to care about one another.

Bonnie's beautiful reddish-blonde hair caught his attention as she positioned herself at the piano up on the dais. His breath caught against his ribs though he wished it wouldn't. Even Ben's prayer hadn't been answered as Sam still had no idea what to do about Bonnie.

He did know he didn't want to add more grief to her life. She'd already suffered enough.

Her fingers moved over the piano keys with ease, filling the chapel with Christmas hymns and a sense of peace Sam couldn't deny. No, he didn't know what to do about Bonnie. But right now, he didn't need to.

He enjoyed the sermon on the birth and life of the Savior. Stood and sang the beloved Christmas songs he'd been singing since boyhood. Sent his own prayer of love and gratitude toward heaven.

Pastor Gray ended with, "Merry Christmas, my friends. May the Lord go with you."

Sam stood as the pastor stepped down from the pulpit and moved up the aisle. With so many in attendance today, and their seats so far away from the exit, it would take a while to get to the preacher, who always stood at the door and spoke to each patron on their way out.

Ben and Rae spoke in quiet voices, their heads bent together. Sam's heart warmed to see his brother so happy, so in love. Sam's jealousy jumped, and he worked to tame it back into submission.

"Sam." Pastor Gray extended his hand to shake Sam's when it was finally his turn.

"Merry Christmas, Pastor," Sam said.

"I have a favor to ask of you," he said.

"Oh?" Sam hadn't done much in the year and a half since coming to Island Park. His work took most of his time, and the preacher seemed to know it.

"An Easter program. I can hear that beautiful voice you have, and I think you're just the person to put together a choir worthy of Easter." Pastor Gray's blue eyes sparkled like diamonds. "What do you think?"

"Uh, sure," Sam said without thinking anything through. He had near perfect pitch, true. His mom had taught all the boys to play the piano too, but Sam hadn't played in years.

Pastor Gray beamed at him. "Great. I already have a piano player for you. You two can work together to build the program. Choose whatever songs you want, and we'll put out a call next week and in our monthly bulletin for choir volunteers."

Sam's head whirred. What had he just gotten himself into?

"Any questions?" the pastor asked.

Sam couldn't think of one. It was like his brain had decided to take a vacation for Christmas.

"Well, let me know if you do," the pastor said. "Oh, here's your piano player. Bonnie, come over here for a minute."

Sam snapped back to attention at the mention of Bonnie's name. Pastor Gray held one of her hands between both of his. His words seemed to echo in Sam's ears as he said, "Bonnie, Sam's just agreed to lead the choir for our Easter program. Isn't that wonderful?"

CHAPTER
FIVE

onnie spent Christmas at her parents' house. It was quiet, and the food was delicious, and the scent of pine trees calmed her soul. She'd loved roaming the forests surrounding Island Park as a child, and she yearned for summer when she could go hiking again.

"How's school?" her mom asked.

"Great." Bonnie smiled at her mom. "How's Dad feeling?" She eyed her father, who had retreated to the recliner in the adjacent living room as soon as dinner had ended. Sitting through the thirty-minute meal had seemed to drain him completely.

"He's tired." Mom wiped the dining table they hardly ever used as Bonnie took the last of the dishes into the kitchen. Worry wormed through her as she loaded the dishwasher and helped put away the leftover ham and scalloped potatoes.

She kept her thoughts silent, but they wouldn't go dormant. She sat on the end of the couch closest to her dad and reached over to hold his hand. "How are you, Daddy?"

A shell of a smile stole across his face. "Fine, baby. How's your boyfriend?"

Anxiety flowed through her as she thought Dad was asking about Sam. She'd mentioned him to them a few times, with hope painting her words.

Then he added, "He still barking at night?" and Bonnie realized he meant Boyfriend the Dog.

Bonnie smiled back at him. "No, I got him all cured of that." She squeezed her father's hand and let go. "I just got him a squirrel toy to chew on. Now he doesn't bark at the critters in my backyard."

"Did you hear about the new fountain going in downtown?" Mom asked.

Bonnie's lungs seized. She had heard about it but didn't want to talk about it. "It's not going in, Mom," she said. "It's being proposed to the city council. They'll have to approve it, and then an architect and an artist will have to be commissioned. It's a year away, at least." Bonnie hoped a lot longer than that. She was planning to attend the city council meeting when the fountain would be discussed, as she didn't want another mother, father, family to go through what she'd been through.

A wave of sadness hit her right in the throat, where she swallowed against it. She closed her eyes and focused on breathing deep. The flickering lights of the television played against the backs of her eyelids. She wasn't sure how much time passed while she relaxed against the couch and let her thoughts run free. But her mom announced, "Time for dessert," so a significant number of minutes had to have gone by.

She heaved herself off the couch, the taste of chocolate and whipped cream already in her mouth. "I'll help." She ran the knife under hot water while her mom pulled the chocolate crème pie from the fridge. Mom sprinkled crushed chocolate cookies on top of the peaked whipped cream, and Bonnie ran the hot knife through it.

An old family recipe, the pie had been a family tradition on Christmas Day for as long as Bonnie could remember. She'd made it for Paul and Jeff every year during the four years they were a family.

With the thoughts of her past at the forefront of her mind, she cut herself an extra-large piece of pie and scooped up the crust bits that fell off the spatula. Mom served a plate of pie to Dad, and Bonnie admired them in that brief moment.

"How long does he have, really?" she asked when Mom returned to the kitchen.

She sighed and took Bonnie's big piece of pie for her own. "He's in constant pain. The doctors say the cancer is everywhere."

"Days?" Bonnie asked, her throat tightening. "Weeks?" Her stomach twisted. "Months?"

Mom looked at her, the same shining hazel eyes as Bonnie's now filled with fear. "I don't know, Bonnie. Could be tomorrow. Could be next Christmas. They don't know. However long he can hold on."

Bonnie cast him a quick glance over her shoulder, her muscles coiling, constricting. She couldn't seem to get a breath. She didn't want to be in this world if her father wasn't. At the same time, she'd known he was going to die soon enough. He'd been sick for a couple of years now.

And you've survived a traumatic death, she reminded herself. For the first few months after Jeff's death, she'd had no idea how to be a person who breathed, lived, functioned. She didn't remember a whole lot about that time, only that Paul looked at her with so much concern in his blue eyes.

Then he stopped looking at her like that. The haze lifted, but if she were being honest, it had never really disappeared. A mist hung around her everyday, all the time.

"Get your pie," Mom said, and Bonnie blinked her way out of the memories. She cut herself another large piece of pie as her mom took her plate with a sly smile and joined her parents in the living room. If this was going to be the last Christmas with her father, Bonnie wanted to savor it.

TIME PASSED QUICKLY, THE WAY IT ALWAYS DID WHEN BONNIE didn't have to work. All too soon, she'd endured a lonely evening at home on New Year's Eve—just her and a handsome host with a giant, glittering ball on the television.

Sam didn't call. Didn't text. Nothing. She didn't expect him to make a personal call or ask her out again. But according to Pastor Gray, he'd agreed to put together and lead the Easter program. She expected him to at least talk to her about that.

Maybe he'd decided not to do it. Bonnie herself had seriously considered backing out. There were dozens of people who could play the piano well enough for the program. The pastor would be able to find someone easily.

Rebecca Frank. Christa Enders. Both of them *taught* piano. The church, and Pastor Gray, and Sam didn't need Bonnie.

She returned to school, ready to fill her days with something good again. All she'd ever wanted was to be a mother, have children. She'd married just before graduating, and Jeff had come along ten months after that.

He'd been her whole world, second only to Paul. And in two horrifying minutes, she'd lost them both.

She straightened as she entered the third grade classroom where she worked. Helping other children had seemed to fill the hole in her life the best. Maybe not perfectly, but well enough.

Her phone chimed just as the bell rang. Bonnie hadn't seen Michelle, the third grade teacher she helped, yet. She checked her phone and dropped it when she saw Sam's handsome face. Her heart catapulted up and then fell to the floor where her phone sat.

The first child arrived with an exuberant, "Hey, Miss Sherman!" and Bonnie bent to retrieve her phone before it got trampled by twenty-four pairs of third grade feet. She managed to shove her phone in the pocket of her slacks, but it burned a hole there until she could sequester herself in the restroom at lunchtime.

Want to get together to discuss the Easter program? Bonnie bent over her phone as if she shouldn't have her device at school. She stared at the letters, trying to figure out how to answer. It wasn't like he'd asked her out. Still, she didn't want to spend any time alone with him. She'd told him right to his face she wanted to kiss him. Hers heated with the embarrassing memory. She still hadn't been able to determine why she'd said that.

"Probably because it's true," she muttered to herself, her lips buzzing with the desire to touch his. Which was so ridiculous, because he wasn't anywhere near the elementary school.

When? she sent. Seemed safe. Non-assuming. Not sweet. Not salty.

Whenever you're available. Evenings are best for me. Are you back at work?

Yes, I'm back at school. How about next week? She didn't want him to think she had nothing on her social calendar, though she didn't. Boyfriend needed a walk in the evening when she worked.

Can I drop off some music? I need some help making a decision on the songs.

Sure, that's fine.

Then we can meet next week.

Okay.

Sam didn't text back, and Bonnie left the safety of the bathroom, her stomach soured against the thought of eating anything. She returned to the classroom, where Michelle ate at her desk.

"Hey," she said glancing up with a smile. She started to look down again but stopped. "Are you okay?"

Bonnie didn't trust herself to speak. Michelle had heard all about Sam last fall. She'd been kind and listened more than talked. Bonnie collected her lunch, though she wasn't going to eat, and her water bottle and sat at Michelle's desk with her.

"Man problems," she said by way of explanation. Michelle would know who she meant. "Don't want to talk about it." She took a long drink of water. "Who are you seeing? Didn't you have a date with Jackson? No, Joel. Joel Jackson." Bonnie finally landed on the right name.

Michelle's pale blue eyes sparkled, but she simply asked, "How was your Christmas?"

Bonnie thought of Sam rescuing her from the runaway horse. The non-date, where she'd practically yelled at him to take her home. The Christmas Day where she'd learned she might lose her father at any moment. He was still alive. Bonnie wasn't sure if she should pray for him to stay alive or pass peacefully.

"No one died," Bonnie finally said, though she'd visited someone who had. "Do you have someone to set me up with?" She needed to get out of her pity party. Needed to get out of her house. Away from Boyfriend, who was aptly named but didn't provide the same things a real boyfriend did.

Michelle glanced back at her lunch, a baked potato with bacon and cheese. "What about Sam Buttars?"

"I'm over Sam Buttars," Bonnie said darkly, suddenly super-focused on unwrapping her cold turkey sandwich.

Michelle trilled out a laugh. "Bonnie, you were never a good liar. Remember that time in high school when the principal called you out of class?" She laughed again. "He wouldn't have known anything if you hadn't gotten involved."

"Someone had to know where that poor pig was," she said in her defense. A small smile formed on her face and she bit into her sandwich. "And I'm not dating Sam."

"Not dating and being over him are two very different things." Michelle speared her with a pointed look.

"He is a maddening, maddening cowboy," Bonnie said. "And now Pastor Gray wants us to work on the Easter program together." She put down her sandwich, her intestines knotted again. "You could play the piano, Michelle." Bonnie leaned forward, desperation coating her tongue. "Would you? Would you play the piano for the church Easter program?"

A horrified look bloomed on Michelle's face. "Just because I played as a child doesn't mean I'm capable of playing for church."

"It's not hard," Bonnie said. "The choir sings so loud anyway." Still, the hope drained away the longer Michelle remained silent. "No one will even hear the piano." Her last words were almost a whisper.

Michelle settled back into her chair. "I think you should spend as much time with Sam as possible."

"What?" A keen sense of betrayal pulsed through her. "I thought we were friends."

"We are." That look came into Michelle's eyes again. That knowing, fierce look. "If you're playing the piano and he's leading the choir, he can't avoid you. So maybe you stay late after everyone else leaves. Maybe there's a kiss up front. Maybe you'll be so hungry after practice, you'll both go to the same restaurant."

"Michelle, come on."

"I'm just saying that he can't walk out on choir practice. We both know Sam won't do that."

Sam's faith was one of his most attractive features. Bonnie adored his dark hair and striking eyes and muscles too. Maybe she should wear her cutest dresses to practices, and lots of pink lipstick, and her best perfume. Maybe some heels. Maybe then Sam wouldn't be able to resist her.

"He's moving to Wyoming in five months."

"And Easter isn't for another three. It's simple, Bonnie. You just make the man fall in love with you in three months."

Bonnie half-scoffed, half-laughed. "*Soo* simple." She picked up her sandwich and took another bite, the conversation clearly over.

A couple of hours later, Bonnie's head pounded like a fist on a door. She'd forgotten how much patience a room full of eight-year-olds required. How much up and down she did for reading groups. How slow the clock moved until it hit three-thirty.

"Miss Carson?" came over the intercom. "Can you send Miss Sherman down to the office for a minute?"

Michelle glanced up from where she was helping a student with their bridge construction. "Yes, she's on her way."

The intercom blipped out, and Bonnie stepped methodically toward the door. She hadn't been called down to the office in a long time. It used to happen a lot a couple of years ago, where there was a substitute teacher shortage in the district and the principal was stuck with classes without a teacher.

This couldn't be that. It was only an hour until the end of school. At least Bonnie could get some ibuprofen in the office before she went back to class. She stalled as soon as she came into view of the office. With a front wall made of windows, the big, black cowboy hat on Sam's head wasn't hard to spot.

What in the world was he doing here?

Fire entered her bloodstream, and she stomped the rest of the way into the office. "What are you doing here?"

He turned toward her, a fistful of sheet music in his hand. "You said I could drop this off."

She didn't miss the way his eyes skated down to her feet and back to her eyes. She was glad she'd worn her black sweater dress to school today, paired with a funky pink patterned pair of leggings, and wedged heel boots. The dress had a gold belt that cinched at the waist, accentuating all her curves. Her hair fell in unintentional waves over her shoulders.

Sam swallowed, and Bonnie suddenly thought that Michelle's suggestion to accept the piano playing position and make Sam fall in love with her was spot on. Judging by the depth of desire in his eyes, he was already halfway there.

He thrust the sheet music toward her. "I was in town and thought I'd drop these by."

She took the pages from him, being careful not to touch his fingers. Some of the fury inside her faded. "Thank you."

"When next week works for you?"

"Any time," she said, her focus on the top hymn. *Christ the Lord is Risen Today*. One of her favorites. They definitely needed to sing that song in the program.

"Monday?" Sam pressed. "I can bring dinner over."

Bonnie abandoned her examination of the music. She lifted her chin and stared him straight in the eye, a plan forming in her mind. "That's not necessary," she said. "Six o'clock at the church?"

She didn't necessarily want to kiss him inside the chapel, but she couldn't have him over to her place and she didn't think he had a piano out at the farmhouse.

"Sure, that's fine," he said.

"Great." She turned and walked away, pausing in the doorway to glance over her shoulder. Sam was still watching, his fists clenched at his sides. She tossed him her flirtiest smile and clipped her way down the hall.

Satisfaction sailed through her. She needed to take control of her life, her future. She didn't want to spend Christmas at the cemetery and with her aging parents. She wanted a home full of love, and laughter, and life. Even if that home wasn't with Sam, Bonnie knew she wanted more than she currently had.

And it was time to go get it.

CHAPTER
SIX

The hours and days until Monday at six o'clock felt like pure torture to Sam. The time felt like it was slipping through his fingers like water, and he wanted to grasp onto it and make it slow down. Because every day that passed was a day he wasn't convincing Bonnie to come to Wyoming with him.

Since Ben had mentioned it, Sam had thought of little else. Would she fall in love with him quickly? Could she? Would she leave Island Park? Could she? Would she like life on a hundred-acre farm in Wyoming? Could she?

Sam harbored a fierce love for the land he'd been raised on, and an itch to get back to it buzzed beneath his skin. He went through the motions of showering, combing his hair, brushing his teeth. He wanted to look and smell his best for Bonnie, and as he pulled into the nearly empty parking lot of the church, he opened the glove box and pulled out a pack of peppermint gum.

A list of songs he'd been thinking about sat on the seat next to him and he grabbed it before he opened the door and let in the winter chill. He flipped up the collar of his leather jacket and walked with all the speed he had toward the front door.

Of all the churches he'd attended over the years, he loved this one the most. A single story with a tall steeple and made of light gray brick, the church possessed a history in its very foundation. He felt the spirit of the place, the love that had been shared here, and the sense of community that surrounded it.

The door was made of a thick slab of knotty alder that he'd helped re-stain with a cherry finish just a few months ago, before the weather turned foul. The arched top seemed to beckon him inside, where he'd find warmth again.

Bonnie's car was parked at the curb, so he expected to see her at the piano in the chapel, and she didn't disappoint. She removed her fingers from the keys when she saw him, but she made no move to greet him. Instead, she watched him with those gorgeous eyes as he approached. He prayed he wouldn't trip over his own feet, and added another plea to the Lord that he could have the right things to say to keep her on the bench. He couldn't believe she hadn't already asked someone else to play for the program.

"Hey," he said as he went up the few steps to the platform.

"Hi." She reached up and shuffled some papers on the

pulpit. "I think we should definitely start with *Christ the Lord is Risen Today.*"

Sam had hoped for more small talk, but he couldn't blame Bonnie for her all-business attitude. He glanced down his list. "I was thinking about opening with *In Christ Alone.*" He glanced up at her but not long enough to make true eye contact. "It has some great lyrics, and we can really amp up the tempo when it says 'There in the ground His body lay….'" Sam sang the rest of the words and they infused his soul with light and life. He took a deep breath and looked up again.

Bonnie gaped at him, her eyes wide and her mouth slightly open.

"We can use the cymbals on 'stands' and 'lost,' I think," he said quietly, a rush of embarrassment heating his face. "Maybe on that next 'I'. 'For *I* am His / And *He* is mine.' Maybe both of those." He drew in a deep breath. "I don't want the program to be loud, but I think it would be appropriate to open with something dramatic."

Bonnie nodded and managed to get her mouth to close. "That sounds like a good idea."

"Can you play that one for me?" he asked.

She cleared her throat and moved more papers around. Her fingers glided effortlessly over the ivory, and Sam marveled at her talent. Sure, his mother had taught him to play the piano, but his hands couldn't accomplish the musicality Bonnie's could. His fingers might land on the right keys, but there was more to beautiful music than just notes. And Bonnie possessed that talent.

Sam's eyes heated as tears gathered there. He followed

along in the music, partly to keep his face hidden, and partly to see where the natural swells and lows were in the song. He marked a couple of things as Bonnie played, and when she finished, he let the final notes linger in the air between them.

"Beautiful," he said, locking his eyes on hers.

Several charged moments passed before she said, "I think that will be a lovely opening to the program." She relaxed her ramrod straight back, and Sam noticed the deep plum dress she wore was nearly sheer and made of something silky he wanted to slide his hand along just before he kissed her.

Struggling to control his thoughts, Sam dropped his eyes to the teardrop necklace that sat against the hollow of her throat. That didn't help his fantasies at all, so he switched his gaze to the stained glass window just behind her left shoulder.

"Are you going to have someone read scriptures?" she asked. "Some other narration?"

"I like sticking to the scriptures," Sam said. "Who do you think we should have do it?" Pastor Gray liked to sit in the audience during the Easter program, and Sam didn't want him to have to do any work that Sabbath day. "I don't know as many people as you do."

"Do you know Larry Kwan? He has a deep voice. Remember how we talked about him that one time we—?" She cut off, her voice muting instantly.

He knew the exact time she was talking about. It was their third date. He'd taken her out to an apiary an hour southeast of Island Park. They'd spent a great afternoon together walking through the beehives and honeycombs. They'd sampled the pure Vermont honey and brought home two bottles each.

Sam had wanted to kiss her that evening. Had wanted to every evening since.

"Larry has a nice voice," Sam said. "I remember I said I wasn't sure who he was, and you introduced me to him that next Sunday. I couldn't believe his body could house that voice."

"He'd be a good choice," Bonnie said. "I can ask him if you'd like."

"Yes, let's do that." Sam penciled Larry's name on the corner of his list. "What do you think about making *Christ the Lord is Risen Today* our finale?"

Bonnie got up and joined him in the theater seats. "What else have you got on your list?"

Sam's brain misfired at her proximity. He couldn't help breathing in the intoxicating scent of her skin, her perfume, her hair. It was a jungle of flowers and fruits uniquely her that he wanted to rub his face in and smell every day.

He gave a slight cough and tilted the paper toward her as she crossed her legs. His brain left his body then, and Sam was only operating on base instinct.

Bonnie gave him a flirtatious smile—the kind she used to flash at him just as she closed her front door when he dropped her off after one of their dates or as she lifted her hand in a shy wave when he saw her at church—and plucked the paper from his fingers.

Good thing too, because Sam didn't think he had the strength to keep holding the list. Nothing seemed to be operational except the involuntary actions of breathing and blinking. She said a few things and made a couple of marks and handed the paper back.

"Well, I have to get back to my boyfriend," she said, stepping around him toward the piano.

The B-word got him moving. And seeing green. "What? You have a boyfriend?" He'd surely have heard if she was dating someone new. Wouldn't he?

Of course you wouldn't, he scolded himself. *You live out in the middle of nowhere with three non-gossipy men.*

Bonnie rolled her eyes, collected the sheet music, and stalked the few steps to him. "Wouldn't you like to know?" She slapped the music against his chest and kept her palm there for an extra heartbeat. He flinched and covered the papers as she drew her hand away.

"See you later, Sam." She shouldered her purse and dang, if she didn't add an extra sway to her hips as she all but sashayed out of the chapel.

Everything inside Sam screamed at him to *go after her. Go after her now!*

But he didn't. He couldn't. He stood there, music pressed against his chest, trying to unravel the storm of emotions swirling inside.

———

"Did you know Bonnie's dating someone?" he asked Ben before he'd even fully shut out the night wind.

Ben glanced up from his position on the couch. He reached for the remote and switched off the TV, leaving the two of them in near-darkness as the only light came from the kitchen at the back of the farmhouse. "Dating someone?"

"Yeah." Sam practically slammed the front door. "She said she had to get back to her boyfriend after only thirty minutes at the church. Then she walked out."

Ben started laughing. He stood up, laughing. Followed Sam into the kitchen, laughing. Leaned against the counter, laughing.

"Stop it," Sam said darkly. "Who could she possibly be dating?" He thought through the men he knew—which wasn't very many. A single waiter at the diner. A couple of guys at the hardware store. He wasn't sure if the man working in the bakery at night was single or not.

Sam realized he'd just thought of four people. Four people who all worked at the only places he visited regularly. He knew nothing of the men at the grocery store, the other place he spent time. At church, he sat by his brothers.

He pulled his phone from his back pocket and shrugged out of his jacket. "I'm calling her."

"Whoa." Ben snatched the phone from Sam's fingers. "Not a good idea." He shoved the phone in his back pocket, which only added red to the green Sam had coursing through his bloodstream.

"Ben," he warned. "Give me that."

"No way." His little brother put his palm on Sam's chest and pushed him back. "You do not wear jealousy well, brother. You're not calling her until morning, at the earliest. Besides, *you're* not dating her. Why do you care if she has a boyfriend?"

"I don't." The falseness in Sam's tone shrieked through the kitchen. "Where are Darren and Logan?"

"Logan's not in from the barn yet. Darren's in the shower."

Sam faced the window, which faced the barns and the expanse of the farm. He wanted to go saddle up and get away from all the walls in his life. The caged feeling expanded as he watched the orange light that glowed above the entrance to the back barn.

It wouldn't be responsible to go riding in the dark, the snow, the wind. Lady, the pure white mare he'd gotten as payment at one of the ranches they'd worked in Nevada, wouldn't like it either. And the bath afterward would leave both of them tired and cranky.

"I'm gonna go fly," he said.

"Oh, come on," Ben said. "Stay and talk about Bonnie's boyfriend!" He added a hearty laugh to the statement, a sound which grated against Sam's nerves as he clomped down the hall to the master bedroom.

He changed into his pajamas and collected his laptop. With his ear buds in and his flight simulator cued up on his computer, he hoped he could lose himself to the intensity and focus it took to land a private jet at the Aspen airport. If he could accomplish that, he'd try a twin engine into Nepal. And then a 707 into St. Martin's. Whatever it took to get Bonnie and her ridiculous boyfriend out of his mind.

CHAPTER
SEVEN

"Michelle." Bonnie stopped short as soon as she entered the classroom. "I did it. I dolled myself up in this old, hideous bridesmaid's dress, spritzed myself with perfume, and charmed the socks right off Sam!" Joy combined with satisfaction and Bonnie couldn't help the carefree laugh that burst from her throat. "It was so amazing."

Michelle burst from her chair. "You did not."

"I did." Bonnie moved to the mini fridge Michelle kept on the counter next to the sink and stuck her lunch inside. "And boy, was he mad when I said I had to get back to Boyfriend. Only I said *my* boyfriend, as if I have one." Bonnie's giggles sounded foreign to her own ears. She hadn't felt this…alive in a long time. It felt good. Right.

"He's probably going nuts," Michelle said, her face beaming.

"I'm surprised he hasn't called," Bonnie said. "Just watch. He'll show up here again today."

Michelle clapped her hands together. "I hope he does."

"I hope he doesn't." Bonnie hung her coat in Michelle's closet and turned toward the crates along the back counter of the room, ready to work. Her euphoria wore off quickly with the busyness of running reading groups and prepping for the afternoon.

Didn't matter. When she returned home that evening, it was with a bounce in her step and a half-smile on her face. "Hey, Boyfriend," she called as she entered the house. Her mastiff poked his head up from the couch and jumped down, snatching up a balled pair of socks before coming around to greet her.

She scrubbed his ears and wrapped her arms around his chest. "Did you have a good day? Of course you did. All you do is sleep on the couch." She stepped around him and deposited her purse on the kitchen counter and slung her coat over the back of the barstool. "Should we go for a walk?"

Bonnie lived about a mile from Main Street, and a stroll there and back would provide her and Boyfriend with exercise—and she could pick up dinner. She changed, layered up so she could withstand the cold, leashed Boyfriend, and set out for the downtown Island Park area.

"Not so fast," she complained as Boyfriend strained against the leash. She trotted a little to keep up with him. Her breath steamed in front of her as she continued her half-jog, half-walk through town.

She finally got Boyfriend to a walk for the last few

blocks so she didn't arrive at the lane of shops, restaurants, and twinkling street lamps too out of breath. Bonnie paused at the end of the street, noticing how quiet it was. The winter crowds didn't usually walk, and because the sun set so early, it felt really late though it was only four-thirty.

At this time, she shouldn't run into too many crowds anywhere. She bypassed the Italian restaurant and The Bean. The diner sat across the street, luring her with the scent of grilled meat, but she stayed strong and continued toward her goal: Pizza Palace. She definitely wanted gooey cheese and sausage and mushrooms tonight.

She looped Boyfriend's leash around a bike rack outside the pizzeria and went inside to order her half-pie and chef salad. "Stay here, Boyfriend."

"Bonnie!"

She paused at the female voice and turned toward the fire station she hadn't passed yet. Rae Cantwell waved, and Bonnie stepped back to the sidewalk. She'd been friends with Rae seemingly forever, as they'd both grown up in Island Park. Their circles hadn't crossed for a while, but she came up to her and embraced her as if they were sisters.

"How are you? Ordering pizza?" Rae reached for the door to the Pizza Palace and waited for Bonnie to enter first.

"Doing great. And yes, today is definitely a pizza day."

Rae chuckled. "For us too."

A stab of longing cut through Bonnie. She glanced at Rae's chocolate diamond ring. "How's Ben?"

"Ben is tired in the winter," Rae said in a somewhat robotic voice, and Bonnie laughed.

"I bet the darkness is hard on the farm."

"It's hard on everyone," Rae said.

"Do you like your new job?" Bonnie watched her friend's face. Rae used to be the recreational youth director, something Bonnie knew she loved. But she'd stepped down last fall, and Bonnie wasn't sure what she did now.

"Oh, yeah." Rae waved her hand like her job didn't matter. "I'm doing mostly the same stuff. It's just not as intense as it used to be."

"Well, that's good." Bonnie stepped up to the counter and ordered her meal. She was told ten minutes, and she let Rae take her turn. Perching on the edge of the seat in a booth, Bonnie was reminded of her high school days, almost twenty years ago.

She and her friends—which included Rae Cantwell—used to get pizza and hide out in the park behind the courthouse. In the south corner there was a set of old bleachers, mostly obscured by the long limbs of a willow tree. They talked about boys they liked, and what they'd do after high school, and how the cook got the pizza crust so perfectly browned.

Bonnie longed for those easier, more carefree days with Rae and Jackie. They'd all left for college, and both Bonnie and Rae had returned. Jackie lived somewhere down the Atlantic Coast, maybe in Maryland or Virginia. Bonnie couldn't remember.

Rae sighed as she sank onto the bench across from

Bonnie. "At the risk of running you off, I'm wondering how things are going with Sam."

"Sam?" Bonnie's eyes rounded. "There are no 'things' between Sam and I. He made that really clear."

Rae's soft brown eyes shone in the dim pizzeria light. "Ben said Sam's been ranting about your *boyfriend*." She glanced toward the window though Boyfriend had flopped to the sidewalk and was snoozing already.

A quick laugh burst from Bonnie's mouth. "Don't you dare tell him," she said, leaning forward, another giggle escaping. "He deserves to suffer a little bit."

Rae grinned at her. "I won't say a thing." She folded her arms. "But who should I say you're dating?"

"Does it matter?" Bonnie asked. "Sam knows about six people in this town."

"He's going to find out your boyfriend is a slobbery mastiff."

"Of course he will. I'll tell him soon enough."

"Tucker and Missy go out there every Sunday."

"So that gives me a few days then." Bonnie's smile grew a bit wicked, and Rae shook her head and laughed.

A twinge of guilt made Bonnie's grin fade. "I'm not a horrible person."

"Of course not," Rae said.

"He...I...."

"It's complicated," Rae said. "I get it. I dated a Buttars too." She gave Bonnie a kind smile just as Bonnie's order was called.

Both women stood, and Bonnie gave Rae a quick hug. "It was good to see you, Rae."

"You too, Bonnie. We should get together for lunch soon."

"Sure." Bonnie smiled, picked up her order, and headed outside to collect her boyfriend.

———

SHE TOOK HER TIME ENJOYING THE MAGIC OF MAIN STREET, but her stomach growled for food and the temperature didn't allow her to linger too long. As soon as she turned the corner where her house sat third down on the left, she saw Sam's truck sitting in her driveway.

Annoyance sang through her for half a second, and then a rush of affection took its place. He really was bothered by her boyfriend. She wondered how long he'd been sitting there, stewing in the cab of his truck.

She knocked on his window, startling him. He exited the truck a moment later, and Bonnie kept a tight hold on her bag of food and her dog. "Did I miss a text?" she asked.

"No." He shoved his hands in his jacket pockets.

"You get lost in town or something?"

Sam glared at her, a silent *no* very obvious.

"Were you planning on waiting here all night? What if I had been out on a hot date with my boyfriend?"

He growled. "You weren't."

She moved toward her front door, glancing down at her dog. "You don't know that." She *had* been out with Boyfriend, but it certainly wasn't hot. The skin on her face felt like it was about to crack, and if she didn't get a bite of pizza in her in the next sixty seconds, someone might get hurt.

She entered the house and unleashed Boyfriend. Very aware of Sam behind her, she dropped her coat on the couch and moved into the kitchen.

"Can I come in?"

She glanced up as if she'd just realized he was still standing there. "I didn't order enough pizza for two."

"I'm not hungry."

"Right." Bonnie eyed him for an extra-long second before pulling out the pizza box and plastic container of salad. "It's not even six o'clock, Sam. You shouldn't even be off work yet."

"It's winter," he said, closing the door behind him, sealing them in the house together.

Boyfriend started lapping at that morning's water, so Bonnie bent to take his bowl and fill it with fresh water. The dog nosed her thigh as she emptied the bowl and washed it out. Dog slobber was so slimy, and it seemed like it never came off. She finally called it good and filled the bowl with clean water.

"Here you go, *Boyfriend*." She faced Sam, cocked her hip, and folded her arms.

He blinked at her once, twice, three times. Then a chuckle bubbled from his mouth. He tipped his head toward the ceiling and filled her house with the fantastic sound of his laughter. If Bonnie thought his singing voice was the sexiest thing she'd ever heard—and she did—this laughter was much better.

Walking away from him last night had been the hardest, and yet most exhilarating, thing she'd ever done. It had been so hard to be in such close proximity to him, listening to him sing such beautiful words about the Savior, seeing the heat in his eyes.

She knew how he felt. She knew how she did. And she wanted Sam more than she wanted pizza. More than she wanted air. More than she'd ever wanted anything before.

So while his laughter still rang in her rafters, she walked over to him, took his cowboy hat in one hand and cradled his face in the other.

Without a word, she tipped up on her toes and kissed him.

His hands came around her, and electricity zipped through every cell in her body. The cool touch of his fingers along the back of her neck, around to her cheek, caused a shiver to trip down her spine. The warm, insistent pressure of his mouth against hers made her muscles weak and everything in the world align.

Finally, was all she could think.

CHAPTER
EIGHT

Sam couldn't stop kissing Bonnie. He'd thought about doing this very thing for months and months. So long. Too long. He hadn't come to her house tonight to kiss her, but he wasn't sorry about it either.

Definitely not sorry about it. His lips felt bruised from how long the kiss went on, and he eventually moved his mouth to her throat and whispered, "I'm so sorry, Bonnie."

"I know you are." The breathless quality of her voice and the way she gripped his shoulders with both hands drove his pulse toward the stars.

Her boyfriend barked, which brought Sam back to reality. He withdrew his lips from her skin but kept his arms around her. She'd dropped his cowboy hat at some point and he didn't even care. He gazed down at Bonnie with such affection roaring through him that he didn't know how to classify it.

"I've wanted to kiss you for months," he said, the words he should've said at Christmas finally vocalized.

Her smile appeared instantly. Sam reached out and tucked her hair behind her ear, such an intimate gesture he'd dreamed about very recently. "So the dog's name is Boyfriend?"

"Yes." Bonnie laughed. "You should've seen your face last night. And tonight."

He gave her his best smile and she leaned in closer to him. "I guess I deserved that."

"I've had Boyfriend since the divorce," she said. "Got him a month after my ex-husband moved out." She extracted herself from his arms and headed into the kitchen to get a plate.

"What was the ex's name?" Sam pulled out a barstool and sat down.

"Paul." She set a second plate in front of him. "I can share."

"It's fine, Bonnie."

"Yeah, I'm going to stuff my face with half a pizza while you sit there and watch." She gave him the stink eye. "Don't be ridiculous."

He didn't argue further but picked all the mushrooms off before biting into his pizza. Bonnie watched him but didn't comment on his fussy eating behaviors. She mixed up her salad with the ranch dressing and ate it all before saying, "You don't like mushrooms?"

"They're a fungus. You know that, right?"

She picked up a piece of her pizza and took a monstrous bite. Sam enjoyed watching her chew it.

Laughed when she said, "Mm, fungus," around a mouthful of food. "Tastes *goood*."

Sam gazed at her, wondering how he could make this his permanent reality. His autumn relationship with Bonnie had never brought him to her house. It had been too young for that, and he'd spent his time with her outside of such familiar walls.

Being in her house felt much more intimate that wandering around an apiary, or eating doughnuts and drinking coffee, or laughing over pasta and garlic bread. And he liked this more intimate setting, because he got to see and experience Bonnie as she really was. Not who she wanted him to see while she played the piano, or while she put on her public face for church, or while she tried to hide her flaws during dinner.

"What else don't you like?" she asked.

"Tomatoes."

"That pizza sauce is made with tomatoes."

"I don't mind it when it's made into something else. Ketchup, sauce, soups, that kind of stuff."

"Strange." Bonnie collected their dirty dishes and left them in the sink. "Want to watch a movie or something?"

"Sure." Sam eased off the barstool and went with her into the living room, where Boyfriend took up two-thirds of the couch. Bonnie seated herself on the other third, leaving Sam to stare down at the dog.

"What kind of dog is he?"

"He's a mastiff. Go on." She shoved the dog's head off her lap. "Get down."

Boyfriend was very obedient, and he leaped to the

ground with a growly grunt. He circled and then sat on her feet, leaving Sam plenty of room on the couch. He'd just kissed her, shared dinner with her, but he wasn't quite sure where to put himself.

"What kind of movies do you like?"

"Whatever." He sat down on the other end of the couch, not wanting to be presumptuous.

"I don't have any of those sci-fi type things. I don't like that kind of stuff." Bonnie giggled, and it sounded nervous to Sam. She nudged the dog off her feet and knelt in front of the cabinet that supported the TV. "In fact, I mostly own romantic comedies."

"That's just fine."

She rifled through the cases and pulled out one with a couple riding a motorcycle on the front cover. "Here's a secret of mine." Her eyes held an edge that really got Sam's blood pumping, much the same way it had been when she'd marched over to him and kissed him. "I like men who ride motorcycles."

Shock traveled through Sam in a single wave. "Wow. I've never ridden a motorcycle. Now a horse? I'm a real pro on one of those."

She stuck the movie into the player and snuggled into his side. Boyfriend leaped back to the couch and filled the other half of the couch with his huge mastiff frame. The dog was obviously attached to Bonnie, and she to him as she stroked his head a few times before laying her hand back across Sam's abdomen.

"I'd like to see you ride a horse," she said as the opening music started playing.

"Come on out to Steeple Ridge this weekend," he said. "I'll show you my lady, and you can bring your boyfriend, and we'll have a great time."

Bonnie laughed and tipped her head back. "Your lady?"

"My horse's name is Lady."

"That's too funny. Boyfriend and Lady."

"Logan has a dog named Rambo. He doesn't like anyone much, except for Logan."

"Does he like other dogs?"

"Definitely. Tucker's got a dog named Fritz, and they get along great."

"So we'll come out on Saturday then."

Sam's chest warmed. He looked into her hopeful eyes and touched the end of his nose to hers. He smiled and kissed her, the very idea of Bonnie out on the farm the most wonderful thing he could imagine.

SATURDAY MORNING FOUND SAM IN THE BARN WITH THE horses though the weekend chores had fallen to Darren. All the brothers usually spent time in the barns anyway, whether it was their assigned day and time or not.

Sam swept the aisles before approaching Lady. "Hey, girl." The horse came over, an eager look in her eyes, and nosed his palm. He stroked the sides of her face with both hands. "Should we have a bath this morning? I have a pretty woman coming out to meet you this afternoon. You should look your best, don't you think?"

He didn't wait for the horse to answer, because horses didn't actually speak English. He didn't put a rope around her neck or anything. She'd follow him down the aisle and into the heated wash stall. Sam had never worked in such a nice facility, and a pang of regret about leaving this high-end farm behind for a broken-down piece of land in western Wyoming pulled through him.

He attached Lady to the lines and turned on the water. Even with the top notch condition of the barn, it still took time to heat the water during the winter. He went through the motions of rinsing and washing and brushing her down.

He loved his horse, and he spoke to her as he worked. "So this is our last winter in Vermont," he said. "I know we've only been here for a couple of years, but there's a great farm in Wyoming that I own."

Lady held perfectly still, not a snort or a snuffle to say about anything he told her. So he talked about Bonnie, because he needed to tell someone and he'd been avoiding Ben, who would surely have endless questions for why Sam had come home so late on Tuesday night.

"You don't care which barn you live in, right?" he asked Lady. "Coral Canyon is a lot like Island Park. You'll be happy there. Lots of big fields. Big mountains. You liked the mountains in Nevada."

Bonnie would like Coral Canyon. He unhooked the lines and Lady gave a little shimmy that caused a smile to grace his face. "C'mon," he said. "Let's go eat breakfast, and later today, we'll go down to the arena."

He put Lady back in her stall with fresh straw and a half a bag of oats. Darren had arrived by then and had half the horses fed. Sam joined in feeding the rest of the animals and met Darren in the back barn when they finished. "Which horse do you think would be best for a first-time rider?"

Darren leaned against the box stall. "Who's riding?"

Sam cleared his throat. "Bonnie."

Darren grinned and grinned. "So Ben was right."

"What's Ben right about?"

"You getting back together with Bonnie."

"We were barely together in the first place."

"Sure." Darren started walking and Sam went with him. "But everyone with even one good eye could see that you were smitten with her." He opened the door and left the barn, exchanging warmth and tolerable light for a chill and the brightest sunshine ever. Sam squinted into it as Darren added, "You still are."

"Yeah." Sam admitted defeat to himself. "I still am." He crunched over the gravel path back to the house, which emanated with the smell of baking pretzels. His stomach tightened and growled. "I hope Ben mixed up some of that honey mustard."

They entered the house and went through the mudroom to the kitchen. Ben had the bottles of ketchup and regular mustard on the counter, along with a bowl of the Dijon-honey mustard Sam had been hoping for. He grinned as Logan came up the stairs along with the clickety-scratch sound of Rambo's claws.

All the brothers gathered in the kitchen, and Sam

swiped his cowboy hat off his head. "I have an announcement."

"A family meeting?" Logan asked. "Now?"

Sam glared at him. "This will take five extra seconds."

"It's good," Darren said. "Let him talk."

"He knows already?" Ben's voice sounded wounded. "I made pretzels this morning for you. I mixed up that honey-mustard you like."

"I'm tellin' you," Sam said. "If you'd just let me talk."

Ben settled one hip into the counter and folded his arms. Logan eyed the hot pretzels on the stovetop, and Darren just grinned that knowing grin.

"I kissed Bonnie Sherman on Tuesday night. She's comin' out here this afternoon." Sam clapped his hands together. "So let's eat. Who wants to say grace?"

"I do," Logan said quickly.

"You kissed Bonnie?" Ben whooped, a gleeful smile appearing on his face.

"You didn't say you kissed her," Darren said. "That's way more than just getting back together."

Sam let the clamoring voices of his brothers fill the kitchen, fill his mind. He smiled at the bunch of them, another pang of sadness infecting his bloodstream. He didn't doubt that moving to Wyoming was the right thing to do. He was simply going to miss this camaraderie. He hadn't been without his brothers for a decade, and he couldn't imagine a home without them.

But the farmhouse in Wyoming would never have this Saturday morning breakfast of laughter, and playful shoving, and innocent teasing about kissing women. Sam knew that, and he allowed himself to feel the sadness the knowledge brought.

Then he dipped his freshly baked and salty pretzel in the best honey-mustard a cowboy could make. Laughed with his brothers. Took the teasing. And prepared to meet Bonnie later that day.

CHAPTER
NINE

onnie hummed to herself as she readied herself for a weekend breakfast with Michelle and Cheryl. They'd promised to order more than fruit smoothies at the diner where they were meeting at nine. Somehow Cheryl had noticed an extra bounce in Bonnie's step—or Michelle had told her about the shenanigans with Sam.

Not that Bonnie had kissed and told. But Michelle had taken one look at her on Wednesday morning and said, "You kissed Sam Buttars, didn't you?" as if Bonnie wore a sign announcing it on her forehead.

Since then, the three had been talking about the next step Bonnie needed to take. She didn't like this wobbly feeling, like she was teetering on too-tall heels. She grabbed her purse and planted a kiss on Boyfriend's head. "I'll be back in a little while, okay? And then we're going to go out to the farm. There's a dog there." She singsonged her last sentence, but Boyfriend flopped to the ground in defeat. He seemed to know when Bonnie was leaving without him, despite her promises to return later.

She arrived at the diner with about ten seconds to spare and found her friends already seated in a booth about halfway back. "I'm with them," she told Annika, the hostess who knew every single soul in Island Park. Bonnie herself had asked Annika about the Buttars brothers when they'd first moved to town.

"Go on back," Annika said, pulling menus from the station and saying, "I can take you back, Harvey," to another group.

"Hey." Bonnie slid into the booth with her back to the front door. She faced Cheryl and sat with Michelle on her right.

"I was just telling Michelle that she needs to have another single-and-searching event." Cheryl took a sip of her water, and Bonnie received her glass from the waitress.

"I know you just got here," Sally said. "Do you need a minute?"

"I'm ready to order," Bonnie said, looking at her friends. When they confirmed they were ready too, she added, "I'll have the French toast with sausage." She hadn't looked at the menu. She didn't need to. She'd been coming to Harry's diner since she was a child, and she'd eaten almost everything on the menu. And maybe had a weakness for French toast.

"I thought you were dating Joe Jackson."

Michelle made a face. "Nope."

"He was interested," Cheryl said. "But Michelle wasn't."

"No?" Bonnie asked. "He's an accountant, right?"

Michelle pulled her silverware out of her napkin. "I can do my own taxes, thanks."

Cheryl shook her head as if Michelle was making a serious mistake. "Anyway, you can't come to the single-and-searching thing, Bonnie."

"Why not? I'm single. I'm searching."

Cheryl rolled her eyes now. "Oh, come on. If I had dreamy Sam Buttars kissing me, I wouldn't be searching."

"He has flaws, you know." Bonnie focused on unwrapping her straw and twisting the paper into a tight rope.

"Name one," Michelle said.

"Two," Cheryl added.

"One: It takes him a really long time to make a decision." Bonnie held up one finger and aimed her sentence at Michelle. "Two." She faced Cheryl. "He has jealousy issues. Three, he barely tolerates dogs. Four, he's never ridden a motorcycle. Five, he's moving all the way across the country in just four and a half months."

She drew in a breath in the resulting silence. Glancing between her friends, she added, "Six, he lives out at Steeple Ridge with his brothers. He barely knows anyone in town, but he's lived here for a year and a half. He's anti-social. A hermit."

Cheryl snorted and said, "Oh, please," at the same time Michelle started laughing.

Bonnie sniffed and folded her arms, glad when the

food arrived, steaming hot and smelling so good her stomach growled.

"Only one of those is an actual fault," Michelle said as she turned her plate holding a Western omelet and reached for the bottle of ketchup.

"Which one?" Cheryl poured raspberry syrup on her pancakes.

"Indecisive." Michelle clucked her tongue. "That's almost a deal-breaker."

Bonnie couldn't help the giggle that burst from her mouth. She opted for maple syrup on her French toast, and she swirled the end of her sausage link in it before taking a bite. The spicy, sweet flavors exploded against her tongue, and everything in her relaxed.

She loved her friends. This diner. Island Park.

But could you love Sam too?

"So you don't think him moving to Wyoming is a deal-breaker?" She didn't dare glance at Michelle. Only when she didn't answer, and Cheryl didn't jump in to say something, did Bonnie make herself look up.

Michelle and Cheryl exchanged a glance.

"What?" Bonnie asked.

"I'm going to say this because I love you, and you need to hear it from someone who loves you." Michelle put her fork down and stared right at Bonnie in that unnerving way she had. "You can leave Island Park, Bonnie. There's nothing holding you here."

"What she means," Cheryl said, jumping in just like she did whenever Michelle said something with a little less tact than was warranted. "Is that there's nothing that *should* be holding you here. It might be good for you to move away. You know, as a way of moving on." She dropped her eyes to her breakfast and cut off a tiny piece of pancake.

Bonnie didn't know what to say. Her parents lived in Island Park. Sure, her older brother had moved away two decades ago, but Bonnie had always loved her hometown and had never felt a pull away from it.

Jeff was buried in Island Park. Her son. She couldn't imagine a future where she couldn't go see his headstone if she wanted to.

She swallowed, her appetite completely gone. She didn't know what to say.

"And I disagree with Michelle," Cheryl said. "I think Sam's got two flaws. The jealousy thing is also concerning." She flashed a wide smile, and the knots that had formed in Bonnie's abdomen loosened and unraveled.

"It's not," Michelle insisted. "It's how Bonnie got him over to her house, where she *kissed him*." She laughed, and the mood lightened further. "Without that, Sam would still be out at Steeple Ridge, spending all his time with his horse."

"Her name is Lady," Bonnie said. The three women looked at each other and sent peals of laughter toward the ceiling. As they settled down and ate, as the conversation moved on to other things, Bonnie wondered how she could leave them behind too. Had they even thought about that?

———

Boyfriend didn't wait when Bonnie told him to. Usually very obedient, she blinked after the dog tearing through the snow toward a black and brown dog on the front porch. That dog barked and leaped off the porch without touching a single stair. The dogs met somewhere on the front lawn and circled and sniffed.

Bonnie watched them with a slip of happiness inside. Sam appeared in the doorway a moment later, wearing that delicious black leather jacket and a pair of suave sunglasses. Without the cowboy hat—which he also wore—and with a big bike next to him, he'd be the picture of perfection.

Her heart still raced at the simple sight of him. Maybe it was time she let go of her bad-boy motorcycle-rider fantasy. Maybe it simply needed to be replaced with a man who rode something with only the power of one horse.

"Hey," she said as she came up the sidewalk. "They seem to like each other."

"Sure do." He leaned against the pillar and grinned at her as she came closer.

Butterflies flitted against the back of her tongue as she mounted the steps, morphing into full-fledged wings when he looped one arm around her and drew her in for a kiss. Bonnie inhaled in the fresh air, Sam's cologne, the scent and taste of toothpaste.

She pressed into him, not able to get close enough. She didn't think she'd ever be able to get close enough to Sam Buttars. Never get enough of the heat from his body. Never get bored from kissing him.

He broke their connection and she laid her cheek

against his chest. He sighed and said, "It's good to see you."

Rambo barked behind her, but she didn't turn. Something squealed inside the house, and she startled a half-step away from Sam.

"That'll be my annoying brothers," he said. "I practically had to chain them inside so I could come say hello alone." He dropped his hand from her waist and turned toward the door. He opened it and said, "You can come out now."

Each of them said something in a low voice to Sam, and Ben looked absolutely gleeful when he stepped onto the porch last. Sam didn't show any emotion, everything contained carefully behind the sculpted mask of his face.

"Darren," one of the twins said, followed by "Logan." While they looked almost identical, Bonnie was well-trained in remembering names and faces. She noticed Logan's eyes squinted more than Darren's, and Logan definitely had a more jovial air about him. His dark eyes sparkled more, and Darren seemed to have the weight of the world in his expression.

Ben didn't introduce himself or shake her hand. He wrapped her in a quick hug and said, "Thank you," before he stepped into Sam's shadow. He seemed to fit there, but at the same time, he really didn't.

Bonnie wasn't sure what to say, but her manners took over. "Nice to meet you. All of you. Officially." She smiled, and for the first time in a long time, the gesture sat on her face without any trouble. With four men staring at her, anxiety hummed in her chest, and Sam finally snapped into action.

"We're gonna go riding," he said.

"Can Boyfriend stay here?" She looked from the frolicking dogs to Logan. "Sam says you're Rambo's human."

"Sure," Logan said at the same time Darren said, "Wait. Your dog's name is Boyfriend?"

"Time to go," Sam said, gripping Bonnie's elbow and nudging her toward the door.

Ben started laughing, and Darren said, "Later, Sam," in a voice that sounded threatening.

Sam herded her inside and closed the door, a long hiss coming from his throat.

"What was that about?" she asked.

"I didn't tell them your boyfriend was your dog." He cast her a wicked smile, and she tucked her hand into his and giggled.

"So, now I get to meet your lady."

"I told her all about you." Sam led her through the farmhouse, which harbored the slightly stale scent of paper, something baked, and…mustard. "She's ready, and she's not the jealous type."

Cheryl's teasing that Sam's jealousy was a flaw entered Bonnie's mind. "I guess she leaves that to you."

Sam pointed for her to go first down a hall and into a mudroom, and he reached around her to open the back door. "I couldn't help it," he whispered. "It burned when I thought of you goin' out with someone else."

He gazed down on her and Bonnie felt stuck in a

trance. Like his eyes hypnotized her, drew her in, rendered her weak. "I guess you kinda like me then."

"More than kinda." He tilted his head and touched his lips to hers for only a moment. "Is that okay?" He didn't wait for her to answer, but kissed her again, longer this time. But not nearly long enough.

Wyoming flashed like a neon sign on the backs of her eyelids. She willed the thought away. She had four and a half months before he left.

And maybe, just maybe, she could leave Island Park too. So she said, "Yeah, I think it's okay," and this time, she stretched up and kissed him for as long as she wanted.

By the time they got out to the barn, a hearty flush had warmed her, and she thought sure his brothers would've timed how long it took them to walk through the house. But she didn't see them. Couldn't hear the dogs barking. Out here at Steeple Ridge, all that existed was peace.

Even the winter wind seemed milder, less of a howl. Sam talked about the farm, the work he did here, and the horses on the way to the barn. He pointed out the hay fields, the show arena, the public parking lot.

"We can board forty horses," he said. "We're full right now. Usually full all winter, from what Missy tells me."

"You've been here for two winters, right?" she asked.

"That's right."

"Does your farm in Wyoming have horses?"

He shook his head as he held open the barn door for her. It took several seconds for her eyes to adjust to the dimmer light inside, and a thrill tripped down her arms at

Sam's touch, the nearness of his voice when he said, "No, it's a regular old farm. Corn and hay and a few animals."

"And you want to do that?"

"It's not about what I want," he said, leading her down an aisle flanked by stalls. Horses clopped and snuffled as they passed. "It's about doing what's right. I loved growing up in Wyoming. I only left to go to college and get a farm administration degree. I was always planning to return to Coral Canyon and take over Dad's farm. He just passed away sooner than any of us planned for."

"I know a little something about that," Bonnie said, surprised the words had come from her mouth. Shocked she'd said them without an ounce of pain in her voice or infecting her muscles. She paused, savoring the moment.

"I'm sorry about your son," Sam said in a voice so quiet it reminded Bonnie of an angel's whisper.

"Me too." She squeezed his fingers. "I'm sorry about your parents."

And though they stood in a horse barn that smelled like dust and manure and wet straw, though there was no radiant light or softly falling snow, Bonnie felt a connection to Sam she'd never had with another human being.

They seemed to move toward each other at the same time, but it wasn't a union of mouths Bonnie sought. Sam drew her into his chest and she went, needing the strength and safety of his arms. He held her tight, but she wondered if maybe she was holding him together too.

CHAPTER
TEN

Sam breathed with Bonnie, finding more comfort with her than he ever had with his brothers. Which made no sense. The bond between him, and Darren, and Logan, and Ben was unbreakable. Sam had made sure of that when he'd promptly returned to Coral Canyon and made sure the four of them stayed together.

While he found acceptance and love with his brothers, Bonnie provided something different. Something more. His heart pinched at the thought of leaving her here in Island Park, and he thought, *I won't do it.*

He wasn't sure if that meant he was in love with Bonnie or not. He certainly wasn't going to say anything now. He'd only kissed her a few days ago. But he'd known there was something special about Bonnie Sherman from the moment he'd met her. Maybe he'd fallen in love at first sight.

Sam wasn't normally so romantic, but his parents had gotten engaged after only four dates. He knew falling in love quickly could happen—he'd just never expected it to happen for him.

"Do you want to meet my parents?" she asked, pulling away from him. She put her hand in his again, and he mourned the loss of her presence right next to his.

"Sure," he said with a shot of fear in his tone.

She heard it, because a knowing smile crossed her face. "They're nice people. I mentioned you to them last fall."

"You did?"

She ducked her head and started walking again. "I guess I kinda like you too."

Sam led her to Lady's stall, his mouth silent but his thoughts rotating. He often needed a few seconds or minutes—or even hours—to sort through things in his mind. College had been difficult for him in several ways, and absorbing information and making something of it was one of them.

"So this is Lady." Sam put his palm against the horse's face above her nose to keep her from touching Bonnie. He could sense the energy of the animals, and apparently Bonnie's nerves too. "She's a good girl, aren't you, Lady?" He cut a look at Bonnie out of the corner of his eye. "You wanna touch her?"

"Where do I put my hand?"

Sam took hers and lifted it, wrapping his hand around hers and pressing his palm against the back of her knuckles. "Right here." He stroked her palm down Lady's neck. "She's a real sucker for a cheek pat too." He moved his hand to Lady's cheek, and her eyes drifted half-way closed. "See? She's a total softie."

Bonnie chuckled softly, and the wonder and joy in the sound erased Sam's anxiety. "I got Lady at a ranch in Nevada where I worked. She was just a filly, but I could see the potential in her. We've been together for five years."

"About like me and Boyfriend then."

Sam nodded. "You'll be ridin' a horse named Dandelion."

"Sounds completely non-dangerous."

He chuckled and dropped his hands. "She's a great horse. Very mild. Darren's been training her for a year. We put all our new riders on her."

She shivered though it had to be close to seventy degrees in the barn. "We're ridin' in the arena," he said. "Indoors. So it shouldn't be too cold."

She smiled up at him, and he had the urge to take her face in his hands and kiss her. Instead, he returned her smile and said, "Let's go get the saddles."

He taught her about general horse care, and how to saddle a horse, and even mentioned how he thought working with horses had healed some of the aches in his soul. She didn't question him on that last part, and he suspected she felt their calming influence too.

In the arena, finally atop the horse, he said, "Can you meet tomorrow after church for choir practice?"

"Sure," she said.

"Great. I'll let everyone know and tell Pastor Gray to announce it too." Sam clucked at Lady and she started walking, her gait even and strong. Dandelion came with her, matching her pace and stride, just the way Darren had taught her to do.

Bonnie spoke about the choir songs, and the Easter program, and told a story about a couple of boys in the third grade class she helped. By the time they ended their ride, Sam couldn't think of another afternoon that had been better than this one.

After the horses had been brushed down and put away, after the saddles had been oiled and hung, after he'd taken Bonnie back to the farmhouse, he asked, "So, do I pass? You think maybe you can trade in your biker for a cowboy?"

She laughed, tossed that beautiful strawberry-blonde hair over her shoulder, and kissed him, the only yes he needed.

Sam's skin itched during church. He wasn't sitting by Bonnie, but in the same pew on the side, on the end with his brothers beside him. He wasn't sure why he hadn't gone down to sit with Bonnie near the front where she liked to worship. He hadn't spoken to her about it, and he wasn't sure if she'd want him to make their relationship so public.

Pastor Gray announced the choir practice and he started his sermon. Since Christmas, he'd been speaking about the qualities that defined Christ, and today's topic centered around Christ as a healer.

Sam's thoughts wandered to Steeple Ridge, to the farm in Coral Canyon, to Bonnie, and back to the pastor's words. Over and over the cycle continued. He managed to catch a few choice snatches of the sermon that warmed his soul and fed his spirit.

He had felt the healing touch of the Savior on several occasions throughout his life. He knew he still had wounds that needed closing, but he'd also learned to trust in the process. So when Pastor Gray said, "The Lord will lead us where we need to go to be healed. Sometimes it's something simple like looking at a rod in the wilderness. Or dipping ourselves in a river seven times. Sometimes the Lord knows we need more than simple solutions in our lives. But I promise you this, brothers and sisters, He knows the solution you need, and He will heal you in His own time."

Tears pricked his eyes, and further down the row, Logan sucked in a tight breath. Sam recognized the masculine display of emotion from his brother. Ben wept when something touched him. Darren clamped his jaw so tight Sam thought sure it would break. And Sam's emotions always came with a quickened heartbeat, a sense of warmth flowing from the top of his head to the soles of his feet, and those pesky tears.

The sermon ended, and Sam dug the keys out of his pocket and handed them to Darren. "I'll find a ride home."

"See you at dinner," Darren said. "Oh, and you should invite Bonnie."

Sam froze. "You think so?"

Darren rolled his eyes, and Sam didn't know if that was

a yes or a no. Logan eased out of the aisle, and Sam asked, "Should I ask Bonnie to join us for dinner tonight? With Tucker and Missy?"

"Yeah, of course," Logan said like such an invitation was as obvious as grass being green. He moved away but didn't make it far before three women surrounded him and started talking. Sam knew two of them, names and all, but he wasn't sure which name went with which blonde. Logan always seemed to attract the blondes.

Ben clapped Sam on the shoulder. "See you at home. Rae's coming to dinner too." They left, and the chapel cleared out, and Sam faced the platform where about thirty people waited for him to direct them.

He had no idea how to direct them, but he drew a deep breath and said a little prayer, and strode down the aisle to join them. Bonnie went up the few steps on the left side as he did on the right, and their eyes locked. They smiled, and it seemed like the lights in the chapel intensified with the energy between them.

Maybe she wouldn't care if everyone in town knew they were dating. Sam cleared his throat and mind and said, "Hello, brothers and sisters. I've got some great ideas for the Easter program."

CHOIR PRACTICE HAD ENDED FIFTEEN MINUTES AGO. Everyone had left, except Bonnie. Sawdust coated Sam's throat. He didn't think he could ask her to the family dinner. It felt like a great big giant step they weren't ready to take.

But he couldn't pretend to be absorbed in the sheet music much longer. And he needed a ride home. She came over and sat next to him. "You okay?" she asked, genuine concern in her voice.

He looked up. "I need a ride home. Do you think you could take me out to Steeple Ridge?"

"You don't have your truck?"

"I share that truck with my brothers. They took it home after church." He straightened all his papers for the umpteenth time. "I'm going to need to buy my own truck when I move."

"I imagine so." She reached over the armrest separating them and stroked her fingers across his before settling her hand in his. "I'll drive you home after dinner."

"Do you cook?"

"Pretty well, yeah. But I thought maybe you'd like to go to dinner at my parents' this afternoon."

The sawdust flew into the back of Sam's throat and up his nose, causing him to cough. The episode passed quickly, and he said, "I'd like that."

"I may have mentioned you were coming when I got home last night. My mother might be making apple pie."

"You stop it right now." His mouth watered.

Bonnie looked at him with alarm. "Stop what?"

"Apple pie is my all-time favorite dessert. My mom used to make it for every picnic we went on. Every birthday. No cakes for us. And she always served it with this ultra-sharp cheddar cheese my dad bought from the dairy farmer on the other side of town." The memories from his childhood, from his last birthday, flooded him, almost drowning him.

Bonnie chuckled and leaned her head on his shoulder. "I don't know if my mom has any cheddar, but I can call her and ask."

"Oh, it's fine," Sam said, his voice thicker than normal. He swallowed. "I like the purist version of apple pie too."

She stood and extended her hand toward him. "Should we go?"

"What time's dinner?" Sam stood and secured her hand in his again.

"Not for a few hours." Bonnie didn't look at him, and he thought she kept her eyes focused on the ground intentionally. "We can hang out at my house, right?"

"If 'hang out' is code for 'napping on the couch,' then yes." Sam added a laugh to the end of his statement, thrilled and comforted when Bonnie did too.

———

BONNIE DROVE A SPORTS CAR. SAM HAD SEEN IT BEFORE; SHE looked sophisticated and way out of his league when she'd worn her sunglasses and put the top down last fall. He'd never ridden with her, and when he got out of the car at her house, he wondered if he should take such risks with his life.

The woman liked to drive really fast, and apparently a stop sign was a "suggestion." He gave her a shaky smile as they went up the steps and into her house. Boyfriend poked his head up from his seemingly perpetual place on her couch, and he flopped back to the cushions when he saw Sam.

"No hello kisses?" Bonnie chirped at him, and he jumped down, scooped up a ball in his jaws, and came trotting around the couch to greet her. "Oh, there you are. That's a good boy." Bonnie gave him a body scrub while Sam watched, slightly amused.

He supposed she felt about Boyfriend the same way he felt about Lady. Couldn't fault her for that, though Lady was definitely a lot less slobbery.

Bonnie busied herself in the kitchen, and ten minutes later she served him a chicken wrap with lettuce, cucumbers, and ranch dressing. "No tomatoes." She sat next to him on the couch, her own wrap dotted with red.

His brain felt soft and tired, but he mustered up the best smile he could. They ate, making small talk about the pastor and his sermon, as well as trading notes on how they thought things had gone at choir practice.

"I definitely think we should do a men's choir with *Jesus Paid It All*," he said. "I'm just not sure I have the male voices I need to pull it off."

"If you used the band—"

"I don't want to use the band." Sam spoke in the kindest voice he could. "I know that song is usually this big rock-out moment, but I think...." He trailed off, waiting for his thoughts to get in line. Sometimes they seemed to take so long. "I think it would bring the spirit if it's just a powerful arrangement of male voices. No guitars. No drums. Just the piano and the voices." He could hear the lyrics in his head, feel the emotion from such a simple arrangement.

"Sometimes less is more, you know?" he asked.

She'd set their plates on the end table a few minutes ago, and now she curled into his side. "Yeah, it's a good idea."

Sam settled further into the couch and leaned his head back against it. He closed his eyes, and breathed in the wonderful watermelon scent of Bonnie's hair. He thought through asking her to come visit Coral Canyon with him, but he dismissed the idea quickly. He hadn't even been able to invite her to dinner at the farm. A trip across the country to see a dilapidated farm? No way he could get himself to make such a request.

But as her breathing steadied and deepened, he fell a little bit more in love with her. He knew he was in serious trouble. He needed help. He just didn't know where to turn to find it.

Her phone buzzed from where she'd put it on the coffee table, but she didn't stir next to him. He let it go to voicemail, but it started vibrating again almost immediately. He leaned forward and saw that her mom was calling.

He started to reach for the phone but drew back. Something inside him whispered to pick it up, so he did. "Hello?" he said quietly, thinking Bonnie would wake any moment.

"Hello?" a woman said, her voice on the upper register of afraid. Sam could practically feel the panic through the line.

"Hello, ma'am. This is Sam Buttars. Bonnie's asleep right now." He spoke in a calm, quiet voice. "What can I tell her?"

Crying came through the line, and Sam gave Bonnie a gentle shake. Her eyes opened, and he motioned with his free hand to the phone. "I'm putting her on the line, ma'am." He handed the phone to Bonnie with the explanation of, "It's your mom."

Bonnie took the phone, a mixture of fear and hope on her face. "Mom? What's up?"

Several seconds passed before Bonnie said, "Mom? I need you to talk to me," the way she would a hysterical third grader. "Is it Dad? Mom?"

Time marched on. Bonnie's face turned white. Her lips shook and became blue. Sam caught the phone a mere millisecond before she dropped it.

"My dad passed away," she whispered as she dissolved into tears.

CHAPTER
ELEVEN

Bonnie wasn't sure how she got to her parents' house, only that it suddenly loomed in front of her. Someone opened the passenger door, and she looked up into the stormy sky to see Sam's face.

He took her hand and guided her up the glistening sidewalk. Had it rained? Was God weeping for the loss of her father?

The numbness that had seeped into her muscles turned into fire, and a sob shook her chest. "Sam," she moaned.

"It's all right, sweetheart," he whispered, his strong arms forcing her to keep moving. "Come on. You can do this."

She breathed, and life flowed into her body. "I can do this."

"You can do this. Your mom needs your help." Sam stepped and Bonnie went with him. They went in the house, and Bonnie couldn't see through all the water in her eyes.

Mom came out of the kitchen, her hands rotating around each other. "Bonnie. Sam." She came forward and grabbed Bonnie in a hug. "He took a nap after church, just like he always does. I couldn't wake him up." She moved down the hall toward the bedroom, and Bonnie breathed, and breathed.

Please help me get through this, she thought, the prayer calming her. Sam's presence at her side further grounded her. She'd been through worse than this. Pulling Jeff from the pond water had been ten times worse than this. Screaming for help when he didn't open his eyes was at least fifty times worse. Walking down the aisle at the church to that tiny, child-sized casket infinitely worse than following her mother into the bedroom and seeing her tired, disease-riddled father sleeping.

"Daddy." The tears had fled, something that never seemed to happen when Jeff had died. She knelt next to the bed and took her father's hand in hers, expecting him to squeeze back. He didn't, and his skin felt too cold. "Sam," she said.

He joined her side and said, "I'm here, Bonnie."

His strength infused her, and she stretched up to place a good-bye kiss on her father's forehead. "I love you, Daddy." She stood and inhaled as much oxygen into her lungs as possible. "Mom, have you called anyone?"

Her mom shook her head, a single tear streaming down her cheek.

"I'll call nine-one-one," Bonnie said. "Then we'll go

from there." She looked into Sam's face, but it held so much pain she couldn't hold his gaze for too long. She walked out of the bedroom, where it had started to smell a bit like death.

She made the necessary calls, informed the paramedics that her father had a do-not-resuscitate order and provided the proper paperwork. They took Dad to the hospital, where someone would be able to pronounce him dead, and store the body until funeral arrangements could be made.

They'd file the death with the county coroner, and she'd be able to get a death certificate in a few weeks. She called Lincoln Torres, who owned the mortuary that had handled Jeff's funeral, and before she knew it, everything had been done.

Everything that could be done at the moment, at least.

"We should go," Sam said.

Bonnie blinked and looked up from where she sat in the hospital waiting room. "Where's my mother?"

He crouched in front of her. "She stayed at home, remember? She said good-bye there." His worries streamed from him, but his dark eyes shone with love and kindness. "Come on, sweetheart. You've had enough for today."

"I can't go to work tomorrow."

"I already called around to figure out who needed to know," he said.

"You did?"

"We've both been on the phone for hours," he said with a quick grin before ducking his head. "Michelle said if you come in this week at all, she'll send you right back home."

"Michelle's not my boss." Bonnie stood and Sam embraced her, held her right against his heart.

"She said she'd take care of it." Sam brushed her hair over her shoulders and ran his hands down her back. "I talked to Ben, who spoke with Rae, who went over to your place and packed a bag. She said I should take you back to your mother's."

Bonnie's throat constricted with emotion. "I want to go home."

Sam led the way, something Bonnie thought she'd be able to do, but couldn't. She watched out the window as the street lamps passed. At the familiar streets. Things streaked past, the same way Bonnie's memories of her childhood, her first marriage, her parents, did. Tears didn't come, but everything inside felt twisted and tight.

Sam took her all the way to the front door and opened it. "Mrs. Gordon?" he called into the house. No one answered.

Bonnie stepped into the house and faced Sam. "I'll be fine."

"Rae said she left the bag…somewhere." Sam glanced around and stepped toward the edge of the porch. "It's right here." He dropped it just inside the house and skated his lips across Bonnie's cheek. "I'll call you tomorrow." Sam touched the brim of his hat and backed away. He turned and went down the steps and the sidewalk.

She closed the door before she remembered he had no way to get back to Steeple Ridge. She flung the door open again, the two halves of her soul ripped right in half. She couldn't leave her mother to sleep here alone. She knew she'd sleep in her childhood home until the funeral, and maybe longer. But she couldn't stand the thought of Sam out in the darkness, the cold…Wyoming….

"Sam," she called to where he stood waiting at the end of the driveway.

He turned toward her just as a truck pulled up to the curb. "I called Ben." He waved and got into the truck. Disappointment dug at her, and she wondered how she'd feel when he packed up everything he owned and moved across the country.

She suspected it would be much worse than watching him drive away and knowing she'd see him tomorrow. She closed the door and leaned against it for a few moments, waiting for the calming influence of the spirit to come over her.

"Thank you for taking him in his sleep," she whispered. "Thank you for Sam Buttars being with me when I found out. Please help me to help Mom." Her voice faded into silence but an unseen strength seemed to fill her muscles.

She pushed off the door and stooped to collect her bag. She'd stay in the guest room next door to her parents' bedroom. She put the bag on the bed and knocked softly on her mom's door. Still no answer, and the house sat in black-gray darkness. She pushed into the bedroom and listened.

The sound of breathing met her ears, and a rush of relief washed through her. She retreated to the guest bedroom, hoping she'd be able to sleep tonight. But the blanket was too scratchy, and the house too warm, and her thoughts so scattered she couldn't put them in neat enough rows to invite the kind of rest she needed.

———

She woke to the smell of coffee and maple syrup. She eased out of bed, glad she'd finally been able to fall asleep. Her mom's bedroom door still sat closed, and the low sound of singing came down the hall from the kitchen.

She found Sam there, flipping pancakes while he sang a song they'd practiced for the Easter program only yesterday.

"Because He Lives,

I can face tomorrow.

Because He lives,

All fear is gone.

Because I know,

He holds the future.

And life is worth the living just because He lives."

Sam put the golden brown pancakes onto a plate and turned to place them on the counter behind him, where he caught sight of Bonnie. He froze, and his beautiful vocals silenced. "Morning. I—I hope this is okay." He indicated the massive spread of food laid out on the counter.

Bonnie anticipated there would be much more food coming that day. It was all people knew how to do when someone died.

"Can I have some of that coffee?" she asked, ignoring

the food. It would sit there all day, and Mom would pick at the bacon and Bonnie would drink coffee and caffeinated sodas all day while she made arrangements.

He poured her a mug of coffee and nudged the sugar bowl closer to her. "Anything to eat?"

"I'll try one of those hot pancakes." She really would try to squeeze a bite or two down her throat for him. He slathered butter on it and pulled the bottle of maple syrup from the bubbling pan on the stove.

"How long can you stay?" she asked.

"All day."

She scoffed as she cut off a piece of pancake. "I know you can't stay all day."

"I talked to Tucker. I can stay all day." Sam beamed at her before loading up a plate with three pancakes. "Have you seen your mother yet this morning?"

"Not yet."

"Did you talk to her last night?"

"No, she was asleep when we got back. I checked in on her." She ate half her pancake and switched to her coffee while Sam consumed half a pound of bacon and nearly all the pancakes, a muffin, two glasses of orange juice, and more scrambled eggs than anyone should eat, ever.

"What do you need me to do?" he asked.

"Let's start with the easy stuff," she said. "The flowers are the easiest, if I remember right. That was a simple phone call. The florist asks you a little bit about who the person was, and it's nice to tell them a little bit about the person. Helps you remember the important things." She smiled though a pinch of pain started in her lungs.

Sam let a few minutes pass without saying anything. He sipped his coffee before collecting his dirty dishes and putting them in the sink. Then he turned and leaned against the counter, his arms folded across his chest.

"I want to be here for you," he said. "I'm willing to give you all the time you need. Honest, I am. This isn't an ultimatum or anything. This is just me asking."

"Asking what?"

"You don't have to answer right now. I suspect you won't even be able to."

Bonnie waited while Sam took the extra time to organize his thoughts into words he could vocalize.

He ducked his head, his cowboy hat concealing his face. "I've been thinkin' an awful lot about you coming to Coral Canyon with me. I'm wondering if you've thought of it. If you think you're capable of leaving Island Park at some point in the future." He lifted his eyes and looked straight at her.

Straight at her with all of his emotions on display.

Bonnie saw hope, fear, worry, anxiety…love. "Tell me about Coral Canyon," she said.

"Don't you have phone calls to make?"

"They can wait." She refilled her coffee and went into the living room, hoping Sam would follow. He did and they sat together on the love seat.

"Coral Canyon is a fun little town in western Wyoming," he said. "It sits right up against the base of the Teton Mountains. Have you ever seen the Tetons?"

"No," she said, letting the sound of his voice wash over her and infuse comfort into her soul.

"They're beautiful," he said. "My dad's—uh, *my* farm sits up near those mountains. The house is old, but I've hired a painter. They were supposed to come in December. I paid them to. I've got new flooring going in this month, and next month, I'm gutting the bathrooms and updating everything to granite."

"Sounds like a lot of work."

"I'm not actually doing it," Sam said. "I'm just funding it."

Bonnie glanced at him and found a fast smile. "I've been paying a neighbor to keep up with the yard, but it'll need some work when I get there. I'm planning to take Lady, of course, and I'd like to maybe get a dog that doesn't hate me."

Bonnie giggled at the same time she gasped. "Oh my goodness! Boyfriend. I completely forgot about Boyfriend." She started to get up when Sam put his hand on her leg.

"I got him."

"Where is he?" She peered at him.

"He's out at Steeple Ridge with Rambo."

"Boyfriend likes you," she said.

"Boyfriend lives in Island Park." Sam stood with a grunt and a long sigh. "What do you think of making your phone calls from Steeple Ridge today? Do you think your mom would come?"

"Let me go check on her," Bonnie said, standing too, Sam's question racing through her mind. Could she leave Island Park? Leave her mother here all alone? Leave the sacred bit of earth where her son was buried?

With every step, she changed her mind.

Yes, she could leave.

No, she could never go.

Yes, she could leave.

No, she could never go.

Yes.

No.

Yes.

She pushed open the bedroom door. "Mom?" For three horrible heartbeats she thought her mother had passed peacefully in her sleep too. "Mom?" She took several steps toward the bed before her mother stirred.

Bonnie froze, more afraid than she realized. "Mom," she breathed. And in that moment, the answer to Sam's question was definitely no, Bonnie could not leave Island Park.

CHAPTER
TWELVE

Sam bagged all the food while Bonnie and then her mother showered. He took them both out to Steeple Ridge, where he hoped they could find some measure of peace and comfort. He'd alerted his brothers, as well as Tucker and Missy, that he was bringing them out there, and Darren had said he'd have coffee and horses ready.

He pulled into the driveway and killed the engine. Rambo and Boyfriend came tearing around from the back of the farmhouse, and Sam chuckled. "See? He's doin' just fine." He slid out of the cab and turned to help Bonnie down. They went around to the other side and Sam kept a firm hold on her mother's elbow as he helped her down.

"We have coffee in the house," he said. "And my brother says he'll let you visit the horses if you want."

"I'd like that," Bonnie said as she drifted away from him.

"Do you want to ride?" Sam asked.

"Can I just feed them?"

"Sure." Sam walked slowly with Mrs. Gordon, who glanced around the farm.

"It's beautiful out here."

Sam took the time to look around. The trees stood nakedly, but they still stood. The snow blanketed what was normally green, and though Sam didn't normally find beauty without blue sky and wide open green spaces, this version of Steeple Ridge was wonderful too.

He could feel a calming spirit here, and he hoped Bonnie and her mother could too. He took them into the house, where everyone—all three brothers, Tucker, Missy, and Rae—shot to their feet.

"Hullo, everyone," Sam said. "Bonnie, you know everyone, right?"

She swallowed and nodded and tears pooled in eyes and Rae rounded the couch and embraced her. Rae took Bonnie into the kitchen and handed her a steaming mug.

"Mrs. Gordon, these are my brothers, Ben, Darren, and Logan. And my boss and his wife, Tucker and Missy." Sam swallowed. "Everyone, this is Bonnie's mother, Lydia."

They accepted her right into their midst, made room for her on the couch, brought her toast and coffee. Missy asked her about the time she'd won a town award for best yard, and that got Lydia talking. She reminisced about her husband, and shed a few tears, and then Logan got her laughing about something.

An hour later, with a bit of food and a lot of caffeine in all of them, Darren said, "It's feeding time," and everyone put on boots and coats and headed out the back door. Sam held back and waited for everyone else to exit before him. He hung in the doorframe and watched his brothers and friends and girlfriend as they walked through the snow, their breath hanging in the air behind him, their voices drifting back to him.

"Thank you for the good people in my life," he whispered. "How am I going to leave these people behind?"

The Lord didn't answer, and Sam didn't expect Him to. Sam had already gotten his answers about moving. He knew it was the right thing. Right didn't mean easy, something Sam was also well-acquainted with.

So for now, he simply caught up to Bonnie, squeezed her hand, and joined in the horse-feeding party.

The week passed in a blur of phone calls, supply pick-ups, food deliveries, and late nights. The day of the funeral dawned with snow and wind, as if the heavens were already in mourning.

Sam dressed in his best black slacks and freshly bleached white shirt. Bonnie had told him that her father's favorite color was red, and Sam knotted a deep red tie around his neck. He added his cowboy hat before leaving the bedroom.

His brothers met him in the kitchen when it was time to go, and Ben pulled out the giant pan of potatoes he'd put together last night out of the fridge. They crammed in the truck and went into town to the mortuary.

Sam's chest squeezed, squeezed, and his emotion teemed so close to the surface. The last funeral he'd attended had featured two caskets and left him an orphan. His fingers shook and he couldn't stop them. Everything in him wanted to bolt, get out while he could, hide so no one could see him cry.

Rae joined Ben, and they walked past the casket and took seats in the back. Darren had frozen in the doorway, and Logan couldn't get him to move. Sam sensed a storm brewing in his quietest brother. He often overlooked Darren because he didn't say much. Got the job done. Worked hard.

From his position next to Bonnie, Sam saw Darren shake his head and spin away. Logan met Sam's eye and lifted his shoulders as if to say, *What should I do?*

Sam didn't know, but he whispered, "Excuse me," to Bonnie and went over to Logan. "Did he say anything?"

"Nothing." Logan's distress was like a scent on the air. "Should I go after him?"

"Only if you want to have a really hard talk with him right now."

Logan sucked in that tight breath that indicated the huge hailstorm in his chest and left the viewing the room. Sam exchanged a glance with Ben, but otherwise could only return to Bonnie's side. Townspeople kept coming and coming, paying respects to Bonnie and Lydia, then pausing next to the casket to pay their final respects to a great man.

Logan and Darren ducked back into the room and slipped into the corner as the seats had all been taken. The time for the funeral drew close, and Pastor Gray stepped into the room to conduct the family prayer.

Most of the room vacated, and when Sam's brothers got up to go with the rest of the townspeople, Bonnie stepped toward the door and asked them to stay. Tucker and Missy too. Rae, and her friends from school, Cheryl and Michelle. Several more women from town—the vet, a boutique owner, a few waitresses from the diner.

Several older men and women stayed, neighbors and friends of Bonnie's parents. Enough people stayed to fill the room, and Pastor Gray started the prayer. Sam let his emotions go up and down, forward and back, hoping the Lord would see fit to inflict just a few moments of comfort on him.

And help me know how to help Bonnie, he added after Pastor Gray had said "Amen."

He shut off his emotions once they made it into the chapel. He couldn't stand to listen to the eulogy, so he lost himself in the list of things he needed to do to make his farmhouse in Coral Canyon habitable. What he'd need to buy when he first arrived at the end of May. The first things he'd need to accomplish.

The funeral seemed to go on and on, and a couple of hours passed before the closing hymn was played by Bonnie on the piano and her mother on the organ. The song was *Because He Lives,* and that made Sam perk up. He'd chosen that song for the Easter program, and he'd sung it at Bonnie's house the morning after her father had died. The lyrics were beautiful, and though no one sang, Sam knew all the words.

Sam stood upon the conclusion of the service, the mood solemn and heavy. The pallbearers took the casket out the funeral doors and the family followed to watch it be loaded into the hearse.

He handed the keys to Darren, as he was planning to ride with Bonnie to the cemetery. Ben went with Rae, leaving the twins to comfort each other. Sam didn't know what to say to Bonnie on the drive over, and the squeak-swish of the windshield wipers sounded between them.

She pulled in and put the car in park, but she didn't turn off the ignition. "I hate this place," she said.

"You do?"

"Most of the time." She stared out the windshield and into the storm. "I do like wandering down the paths in the middle of summer. It's green, and peaceful, and the breeze is welcome then."

"Do you come to visit him often?"

"Jeff?" Bonnie finally swung her eyes toward Sam. She wore a lot of makeup today, and she hadn't cried yet. Sam wondered if she would. She didn't seem to have any problem talking about her son either.

"Yes, Jeff. Do you come visit him often?"

"He's not here," she said. "Sometimes I visit the gravesite, but I don't imagine him to be there."

"No?"

"No. I can't fathom the thought of him spending his time here, especially in such a dreary place." A haunted smile crossed her face. "I like to think of him somewhere full of light, with rainbows, and sailboats, and horses. He liked rainbows, and sailboats, and horses."

"So…." He cleared his throat. "And I don't mean to be insensitive, but why visit the gravesite?"

"Have you never visited your parents' final resting places?"

Sam shook his head, the lump in his throat immediate and thick. "No," he managed to say.

Bonnie sucked in a breath in a whoosh. "Well, I can't speak for everyone, but for me, when the memories are a bit overwhelming, I go to the cemetery. I give them a few moments to take over my life. Then they…fade again, almost like the grave siphons them away."

"You don't want the memories?"

"I want to *control* the memories."

Sam didn't understand, but he didn't press her further. "Should we go?"

"They won't start without me," she said with a sigh. "But I suppose we should go."

Sam stepped from the car and opened his umbrella. He hurried around the hood and held the umbrella over Bonnie as she got out. They shared the protection from the sleety snow and joined the rest of the group gathered at the gravesite.

More words were spoken. Another prayer said. Bonnie explained that her father wanted a balloon send-off, but because of the weather, she'd be planning one for that summer.

Sam turned and started wandering away after that. The end of his patience had nearly arrived, and he hated the way Bonnie had announced to everyone there that she'd be here in the summer.

Here. In Island Park.

Not with him in Wyoming.

The snow saturated his shoulders, but his cowboy hat kept his face dry. He didn't chart a course, but simply let his feet take him where they wanted to go. He hated cemeteries for about the same reason as Bonnie. No one ever came to one to celebrate. No one hosted a party at a cemetery. Everyone who came wore sadness like perfume and the very air held the misery captive.

Soon enough, he stood on the edge of the cemetery and faced Steeple Ridge. He could just make out the barns from here, across the nearly half-mile of pastures and hay fields that sat between him and the horse he suddenly wanted to see.

Lady would bring him comfort on this day unlike anything else. Maybe not the Lord and maybe not Bonnie, but both of them seemed to be absent at the moment. He didn't like thinking about the day his parents died. Didn't want to admit to anyone, even himself, that he'd taken an interest in the flight simulator so he could learn how to land the plane they'd died in. Didn't want to imagine how his life would be different if they'd simply made it to Aunt Annie's, visited her and her new baby, and come home.

Would he even own Lady? Would he have been back at the farm by now? He never would've met Bonnie, and he turned as delicate footsteps approached.

"Sam?" She came to his side and slipped her icy fingers into his.

"You're cold," he murmured.

"It's done," she said in response.

"Now what?" he asked.

"The ladies from the church have put together a luncheon. We'll go back to the church and eat."

Sam nodded, but the last thing he wanted to do was spend more time with people. He'd do it, though. For Bonnie, he'd do it.

She moved in front of him and brought her free hand to his face. He looked down at her, the simplest of touches making his breath catch. He hadn't kissed her in days, the emotional turmoil not much of a backdrop for romance.

He wouldn't kiss her now, either. Cemeteries weren't built for kissing.

She stretched up and matched her mouth to his. He yearned to give in to her touch, but he cut the kiss short by ducking his head and grinding the emotion out of his throat. "Bonnie."

"Did you come this way on purpose?" she asked.

"Just walked."

"Jeff's grave is right back there."

Sam glanced over his shoulder. "I should've known. I'm sorry."

She took his hand and stepped slowly toward her son's headstone. "I've been thinking about what you asked me."

Sam kept his eyes on the ground, unsure of how to answer. He didn't want to seem too eager, but he certainly didn't want to open his heart and then have it get stomped on.

"On days like today," Bonnie said. "I would gladly leave this town, go anywhere you want."

His eyes flew to her face, but she didn't look at him. "Anywhere I want?"

She paused at the end of the row and glanced down to Jeff's. "To Coral Canyon, Sam." She looked at him, her eyes locking onto his. He couldn't look away, not that he wanted to. He could get lost in hazel eyes like Bonnie's, so soft and fierce at the same time.

"I'd go with you to Coral Canyon, Sam."

His brain couldn't handle such a powerful statement, though it was only a few words long. So he simply leaned down and pressed his lips to hers, an acceptance of what she'd said. Of who she was. Of what she had to offer him.

CHAPTER
THIRTEEN

As Bonnie kissed Sam, she wanted nothing more than to leave Island Park. Put it in her rearview mirror and never come back. But she still had a funeral luncheon to attend and dozens of meals to pack up and put in her mother's freezer. They'd all be thrown away eventually, but Bonnie would put on a sunny smile and infuse as much gratitude into her voice as she could. She'd tell people she was fine, when really her entire reality had changed.

She knew death did that. It changed a person. Altered the course of their life. After all, one could not simply go on as they were after someone they loved departed.

So she went back to the church with Sam. Accepted the condolences. Kept a watchful eye on her mother. Left as soon as she was able, Sam at her side. Sam always at her side, except for those few minutes in the cemetery. She hadn't noticed when he'd left, and she'd found him easily enough.

He endured the crowds as well as she'd hoped he would, but he wore the relief plainly on his face once they got to her car. He went to her mother's with her. Helped her put away the extra food, sat with her on the couch until she fell asleep.

When she woke the next morning, the house felt empty. Sam had gone, and Bonnie pulled herself from the sofa and worked the kinks out of her muscles. It was the Sabbath Day, but the thought of going back to the church made her throat dry and her hands sweat.

Hours passed and turned into days. She went back to work, where Michelle watched her with worried eyes but the kids didn't treat her any differently. She gravitated toward them, because she wanted to feel as normal as possible. Days went by, and Bonnie struggled to arrange a new schedule where she stopped by her mother's after work each day, spent time with Boyfriend, and called Sam before bed.

The phone calls were his idea, and though sometimes their conversations only lasted four minutes, he claimed he wanted to hear her voice each night. He always asked her how she was, and he'd said, "And don't lie to me. I'll be able to hear it," several times.

A week passed, then two, and Bonnie couldn't bring herself to return to church for the sermon. She arrived late and stayed in the car until people started coming out. Then she'd go in and take up her seat at the piano.

She wasn't sure why she could do that but couldn't sit

on a bench and listen to Pastor Gray. She adored the man; he always said at least one thing each week that buoyed her up for another week of work and winter.

As January gave way to February, the Easter program had been solidified. Sam still didn't have enough male voices for the rendition of *Jesus Paid It All*, but he claimed to be working on it.

Valentine's Day arrived, one of the most dreaded days for singles everywhere. Michelle had set up her single-and-searching event for that night, but Sam had asked Bonnie to dinner. She'd said yes, of course, and she fed Boyfriend early and put on a teal dress she hoped didn't clash terribly with her hair.

She wore tights to stave off some of the chill and slipped on a pair of chunky heels right as the doorbell rang. She giggled at Sam's formality though Boyfriend barked at it. She answered the door and cocked her hip with a smile on her face.

Sam grinned at her, the sight of him stealing her breath and accelerating his heartbeat. "Evenin', sweetheart." He held a bouquet of red roses and put them behind her back as he leaned down and kissed her. She detected something new in this touch, but she couldn't quite identify what it was.

He wore a pair of gray slacks and that sexy leather jacket with a hint of a blue collar under that. "Can I come in for a minute?" He crowded into her house without waiting for her to answer.

She took the roses from him and inhaled the scent of them. Her blood rushed faster through her veins with the floral scent—and the touch of Sam's hand on her back. "You look beautiful," he said.

"Thanks." She clomped into the kitchen with her huge sandals. "You look absolutely delicious."

He chuckled and leaned against the counter while she filled a vase with water and poured in the flower food granules. "I'm not sure what that means, but I'll take it."

She pressed into him, fisting the collar of his jacket in her fingers. "It means you look good enough to eat." She kissed him, deepening their kiss the way her feelings for him had deepened.

He went with her, holding her close and kissing her like a man in love. All at once, she knew what the change in his kiss was. Love.

Sam loved her.

A smile slipped across her lips, breaking their connection, and she giggled. "That was nice. You're a very good kisser, Mister Buttars."

He growled, the edge in his dark eyes almost dangerous, and kissed her again. With Paul, she'd fallen slow and steady as he revealed one piece of himself to her at a time. But she knew what falling in love felt like. She was just doing it faster with Sam. A lot faster.

She expected fear to fill her, but it didn't. Maybe it was the perfect pressure of Sam's mouth. The warmth spreading through her, originating from his hands in her hair, along her face. The spiraling sensation of love rising through her.

He finally pulled back and lifted his head, tucking her into his chest. His heart beat against his breastbone, a fast thudding that radiated through Bonnie's face. He breathed in and out, in and out, quickly, and she experienced another moment where she'd leave Island Park and follow this man anywhere.

"So, dinner?" he finally asked, his voice husky and throaty and sexy.

"If we have to."

"I have a reservation," he said. "You don't want to eat?"

"I want to." She tipped up and kissed him again. "I want to do this too, though." She wasn't sure what was so intoxicating about him tonight. Maybe she simply hadn't had a date on Valentine's Day in five years. Maybe she just needed him more than she'd thought at this time, only a month after her father's death.

Or maybe she was already farther in love with Sam than she thought.

————

THIRTEEN DAYS PASSED BEFORE SAM SHOWED UP AT BONNIE'S house again. She spent lots of time out at Steeple Ridge, the only place that seemed to bring her any measure of comfort. She took Boyfriend out for his doggie playdates, and spent hours with Dandelion, Sam, and Lady. Darren always seemed to find them with his horse, Paintbrush. The paint pony looked like each of his hooves and his tail had been dipped in red-orange paint and then someone had splattered the paintbrush over his beige body.

He eyed Bonnie for the first few days, but then he clopped on over to her like they were old friends.

"I come bearing garlic bread and chocolate covered caramels," Sam said when Bonnie opened the door.

"Two of my favorite things." She leaned up and kissed him. "Make that three." She grinned, happier than she could ever remember being, and stepped back to let him enter the house. Boyfriend came trotting over to sniff the food, then sat as if his obedience would earn him a bite. Truth be told, it probably would.

Sam bent down and scratched the dog behind his ears. "Hiya, Boyfriend." He moved into the kitchen, where he set much more than simply garlic bread on the counter.

"What else did you bring?"

"Those spinach stuffed shells," he said. "And a sampler of the ravioli you alluded to last week."

Bonnie got down plates as she asked, "You brought the sheet music?" The practices for the Easter program had been going well, but Sam wanted to do a different arrangement for *The Old Rugged Cross*. He'd convinced Zoey Stephens, one of the best sopranos in town, to sing the solo part, and he wanted the accompaniment to match her intensity.

Bonnie was proficient on the piano, but she needed extra practice with the song in order to match Sam's vision. And if he brought her pasta and buttery bread as part of the deal? Nothing could be better.

"I left it in the truck." He glanced around. "Where's your piano?"

"In the guest bedroom." Bonnie scooped two ravioli

and a shell onto her plate, going back for some of the housemade marinara sauce. Everything with Sam felt comfortable now, including slurping spaghetti and consuming large amounts of garlic. She'd kiss him later, and he wouldn't even complain.

She took her food to the couch, where he joined her with Boyfriend lying obediently a foot or two away.

"So there's something I want to ask you," Sam said, his head bent away from her gaze. She recognized this tactic. The question would be emotional, hard for him to ask, and even harder for her to answer.

She took a big bite of bread. Chewed real slow and swallowed. "Okay."

He looked up, those eyes serious and absolutely sinful. The intensity within them never failed to surprise her. "I'm just wondering how you feel about having more children."

A thin layer of ice coated everything inside Bonnie. Her stomach squirmed, and her heart struggled to beat. When it finally broke through, it hammered like someone had injected a double dose of adrenaline right into her chest.

"I don't have to know right now," Sam said. "And I completely understand if you don't think you can—"

"Do you want kids?" she asked.

Sam's throat worked as he swallowed. It looked painful, and a twinge of discomfort stole through his expression. "I don't want my answer to influence yours."

Bonnie had never entertained the idea of having more children. Of course, she'd never thought she'd remarry either. Hadn't dated in years and years. No one in Island

Park had really tried to take her out, and no one had been remotely interesting—until Sam.

She thought of Jeff, with his reddish hair and smattering of freckles. He'd been her whole world, and even with Paul she'd never felt like she needed to expand their family. She was a decade older now than she'd been when she had Jeff, and she honestly didn't know how she felt about having another child.

"I don't know," she finally admitted. "I've never really thought about it." The fact that he was thinking about it meant he was thinking long-term. Thinking seriously long-term.

He nodded and went back to his food. "Something to think about then."

"I want to know what you think."

He finished his food, taking a few minutes the way he always did. At first, his habit had been annoying, and she'd found him a bit indecisive. But now, Bonnie appreciated the maturity and care with which Sam gave his attention to important matters.

"I'd like children," he said real quiet, like he was afraid to jinx something by speaking too loud. "Maybe not four boys in five years, but a kid or two whenever we're—" He cleared his throat. "Whenever," he finished with a thick tick of emotion in his voice.

The silence between them turned charged, and Bonnie didn't know how to release the pressure in the air. She crunched through the last of her bread and stood up, collecting his plate and taking it into the kitchen with hers.

"I'll get the music," he said, practically running from

her house. He took an exceptionally long time returning, almost like he needed to drive all the way back to Steeple Ridge to collect the music.

He ducked back inside without knocking, and Bonnie led him down the hall to the den-slash-music studio. "Tell me what you want again."

"So Zoey can control the tempo," he said. "I thought what she did on Sunday was nice."

Bonnie spread the music out and sat on the bench, adjusting it as she hadn't played here in a while. "I remember," she said. "I marked it." She took a few seconds to study the music, looking for her tempo marks. "You want me to match those?"

"In tempo and volume. I think she can carry the song, and I think it's powerful to let her."

Bonnie straightened her back. "Do you want to sing while I play?" The sound of his speaking voice infused her soul with peace, and when he sang, Bonnie imagined the hosts of heaven singing just for her.

He came and stood behind her right shoulder. "Yeah, I can do that."

She put her fingers on the keys, calming the slight tremor in them so she could play with confidence. She took a deep breath, prayed for a quick beat, and began playing.

He sang in his flawless tone, swelling where Zoey had and pulling back in the exact spots Bonnie had marked.

Bonnie finished the last few chords and let the music hang in the air. Her soul rejoiced at the idea of clinging to Christ until the end, the way her father had done. Rejoiced at being reunited with her Savior someday. Rejoiced that her pain and iniquities had been pardoned and sanctified through the sacrifice of the Lord.

Not until a drop of wetness splashed on her collarbone did she realize that she'd started crying. Sam lifted his leg over the piano bench and she scooted down to make room for him. "I think that was darn near perfect, Bonnie."

She leaned into him, glad when he lifted his arm and draped it over her shoulders, cradling him against his side. "I think *you're* darn near perfect, Bonnie."

She smiled, and a quick laugh came out of her mouth. "We all have flaws, Sam."

"Yeah, you burnt that toast last week."

"That was *not* burnt," she said. "You and your brothers like warmed bread."

"We can't get the charcoal smell out of the farmhouse." He chuckled and pulled her closer, tighter.

She shouldered him, her affection for him growing despite the teasing. They really didn't know what the definition of "toast" was. She'd cranked the setting on their toaster from the two to the seven, and actually shown them what toast looked like. Not a one of them had eaten more than a couple of bites.

"How are you feeling about Coral Canyon?" he asked. He'd checked in with her a few times since her father's funeral, and he always seemed to ask when she was feeling particularly close to him and far from everyone and everything in Island Park.

"When are you going again?"

"Next weekend. It's a fast trip. I'm leaving after choir practice and coming home Wednesday morning."

"I don't know if I can take off three days of work."

"Something else to think about," he said. "No pressure."

He'd explained several times that he just wanted her to come see the town. He was convinced that if she'd go to Wyoming, the magic of the place would infect her and she'd be more willing to relocate.

With only two months until Sam made the move, Bonnie wondered if a simple visit would be enough. She thought there should be diamonds and vows and a long, white dress before she moved to Coral Canyon.

But a visit couldn't hurt, could it?

"I'll go," she said.

"You want to check with your boss on Monday?"

Bonnie shook her head. She'd go whether she had the time off or not. "Can you forward me your flight information? I'll book something as close as I can."

"No need," he said, standing and heading for the hall-way. "I booked two tickets with the hope you'd say yes." With that, Sam ducked into the hall, leaving Bonnie to marvel at his quiet strength, his unwavering faith, his appalling nerve.

CHAPTER
FOURTEEN

Sam's nerves fired like a faulty engine. His heart skipped every third beat as he parked in Bonnie's driveway and walked up her front steps. They were going on a trip together, something Sam had never done with a woman. Ever.

He'd double and then triple-checked the itinerary, making sure they had time for dinner after the flight, and breakfast before the return flight. He'd over-packed, not sure what to expect while they were in Coral Canyon. Which was absolutely absurd, because it was the middle of March in Wyoming, and he certainly didn't need shorts or swimming trunks.

His suitcase held both, and a flash of foolishness snaked through him. Bonnie looked up from her position in the kitchen. "Hey." She smiled and nodded toward him. "My bag is right there."

She had a sensible carryon-sized bag by the front door.

Sam took it and left the house again, unsure of why he felt like the ground was about to disappear beneath his feet. Probably because Ben had said, "This is a big step, Sam." And Darren had promptly agreed, saying that he hoped Wyoming would be on its best weather behavior.

Sam had checked that too. Supposed to be cold but clear the whole time they were visiting Wyoming. He put her bag in the back of the truck and faced the house. She came out a few seconds later with Boyfriend, who bounded down the steps and toward the tailgate.

"Up you go," Sam said, and Boyfriend leaped into the truck bed. Sam went around to Bonnie's door and opened it for her, skating his hand along her back as she passed. She handed him a box with her dog's food and toys. When she glanced up at him, something hot and charged passed between them.

Sam couldn't seem to find much to say as he drove back to Steeple Ridge so Boyfriend could stay with his brothers and Rambo. Logan waited for them on the front porch, only standing when Sam got out and retrieved the box from the back. Boyfriend went flying from the truck, and Sam handed the box off to Logan.

"So you're really doing this," Logan said, a question nowhere in his voice.

"I'm nervous," Sam said under his breath. "What if this doesn't go well? What if she hates Coral Canyon?"

Logan kept his eyes on the truck for an extra heartbeat. "Well, we know she likes you, Sam." He clapped his hand on Sam's upper arm. "So just be your charming self and everything will be fine."

But Sam wanted more than fine. He wanted magical, exciting, adventurous. He returned to the truck and said, "Shall we?"

"We shall." Bonnie gave him a great big grin and he got the truck back on the highway. Once out of sight of Steeple Ridge, she slid across the seat and put her hand in his. "Tell me about the farm again."

Grateful for words to say, Sam detailed the fields, the garden, the house. He spoke about his parents and their love and care of the land. The two-hour drive to New York City passed in a blink, and Sam finally relaxed once they'd made it through security at the airport.

"It'll be dark when we get in," he said. "But I'll come pick you up first thing in the morning. We'll go on a grand tour of the town." He pointed toward a row of eateries. "You want to eat before we go to our gate?"

She did, and once they had their food and had found somewhere to sit, he said, "Bonnie," in a way that made her jerk her head up.

"Yeah?"

He'd ordered these words before, but they scrambled inside his throat as he prepared to say them. So he took another bite and commanded his thoughts to assemble themselves. A minute later, they did, and he continued with, "I'm real glad you're coming to Wyoming with me."

The tension on her face melted. She reached across the table and squeezed his hand. "Me too."

"I'm wondering if you might want to tell me a little bit about your son on the way." Sam wanted to know everything about her, and while she'd given him little details about her ex-husband and her life before he'd arrived in Island Park, most of it was still a giant black hole.

No wonder, he thought as unadulterated panic paraded across her face. "I mean, when you're ready," he added.

She swallowed and put her fork down. "I forget that not everyone knows about Jeff."

"I haven't even seen a picture of him," Sam said. "You don't have any around the house."

"Sure I do," she said.

"I haven't seen one."

"In the den," she said. "There's one in there."

Sam had only been in her den once, and he hadn't examined every picture on the walls or end tables. But he hadn't seen a picture of her son. "All right," he said anyway.

"It's a very painful thing," she said. "Thinking of him. Talking about him. Imagining what he'd be like today if he were still alive."

He had no idea what it felt like to lose a child, but they'd had plenty of conversations about losing a parent. He did understand loss on some level. Had endured extreme mental and emotional anguish. Had given a lot of thought to life after death, and spent a fair bit of time wondering how his life would be different had his parents not passed away.

"I understand." He didn't want to push her away, or give her a reason to retreat. Bonnie had met most of his questions head-on, with honesty and heartfelt answers.

They finished eating and Sam directed them to their gate. Amongst the hubbub of the Sunday afternoon travelers, Bonnie tucked her feet underneath her and leaned toward Sam. "Jeff was only four when he died. He drowned in the pond at the sports complex."

Sam threaded his fingers through hers and held on tight. She put her other hand on top of their entwined fingers. "I'm sorry."

"I've thought a lot about what he must have felt in those last moments of his life." She shivered though the airport was overcrowded and definitely not cold. She gave a little shake of her head. "I was talking to a friend of mine, and he was chasing a soccer ball. It had gone in the pond and he went in after it. I—I don't really know what happened after that. He'd had swimming lessons and knew how to float." Her voice weakened until her last word was practically a whisper.

An apology was completely inadequate, but Sam didn't know what else to offer. His silence felt inconsiderate. "I can't imagine," he said just to have something to say.

"Jeff liked sailboats. He liked my mother's strawberry rhubarb jam. His favorite colors were blue and green, because dinosaurs were blue and green." A haunted smile graced her face. She didn't say anything more, and Sam let the subject pass. She'd told him a few things, and he'd take the information in bite-sized pieces until he'd heard it all.

———

A FEW HOURS LATER, SAM STOOD AT THE CAR RENTAL counter with Bonnie beside him. His earlier anxiety bounced through him again no matter how he tried to coach himself that *everything would be fine*. He'd forgotten about the time difference, and it wasn't nearly as dark as he'd thought it would be.

"So it's a two-hour drive," Sam said. "I think I mentioned that?"

Bonnie yawned. "You did. And you mentioned something about getting the best hot dog in the state at the gas station."

Sam chuckled. "That I did." He managed to fill the time with small talk, arriving in Coral Canyon a few minutes after six o'clock. He pulled up to the gas station, which a man his father's age owned. George stood behind the counter, the way he always seemed to. His face lit up when he saw Sam.

"Sam." He shook the man's hands, his eyes roaming to Bonnie. "And you must be Bonnie."

Sam cringed, forgetting that he'd bemoaned about his romantic misadventures before Christmas. How George had remembered Bonnie's name was phenomenon. "Bonnie, this is George. He's an old friend of my father's."

"We grew up here in Coral Canyon." George said. "My oldest is the same age as Sam's youngest brother, Ben."

"Nice to meet you," Bonnie said. "Sam mentioned something about an amazing hot dog...." She glanced around.

George chuckled and stepped around the counter. "That'll be the all-beef foot-long. I recommend the special sauce and a big scoop of chili."

Bonnie followed him over to the hot dog cooker, which rolled the delicious dogs until they were glistening and golden brown. "Do I look like a chili dog kind of woman?"

George fell back a step. "Do they not eat chili dogs in Vermont?" He shot a look at Sam, who raised his hands as if to say, *You're on your own.*

"I'm a bit of a purist," Bonnie said, taking out a bun and reaching for the tongs. "But tell me about this special sauce."

"It's ketchup mixed with mayo," George said.

"I can put that and mustard?"

"Sure."

Bonnie nodded and set about creating her hot dog. George returned to where Sam still stood at the counter. "I like her," he murmured, and Sam grinned as he moved to make himself a hot dog too.

They ate their hot dogs and chips in the car in the parking lot of the high school, the way Sam had as a teenager. Then he drove toward the mountains, taking the main street filled with shops and galleries and other touristy hot spots. Bonnie's head seemed to be on a swivel, and she asked questions about the size of the town, and how tall the mountains were, and how the town could support two grocery stores.

Sam liked telling her about Coral Canyon, enjoyed that she seemed as entranced by it as he was. Maybe she really would move here with him.

His mind immediately started spinning with all that needed to be done before that could happen. He'd need to tell her how he felt about her. Find out if she felt the same. There was a ring to buy and a wedding to plan, and there was also absolutely no way any of that would happen in the next two months.

With every day that passed, Sam had tried to admit that she wouldn't be moving to Coral Canyon with him when he did at the end of May. He'd spent an unhealthy amount of time considering what *would* happen, and he never liked what he came up with.

His tongue felt thick in his mouth as he turned the corner and continued out of town to the farm he owned and would soon be operating. He pulled into the gravel driveway with a strip of grass between the tire tracks. Well, there would be if the ground wasn't covered with snow. Someone had been to the house, though, because the snow had been driven on and packed down.

The blue house sat before them in the dusky light, and Sam peered at it. "So this is the farmhouse."

"It's big."

Sam didn't know what that meant. If it meant anything. He didn't think the house was particularly big, but maybe Bonnie had thought he'd be living out in the middle of nowhere in a tiny shack. He suddenly didn't want to take her inside, but she reached for the door handle and got out of the rental car before he could say anything.

He hurried to follow her, taking her hand and leading her toward the entrance on the side of the house. These stairs had been cleared, and he stuck the key in the lock to get the door open. "So this is the entrance we used the most," he said, his voice hardly his own. "If someone came to the front door, it was for piano lessons or a visit. Even then, my mother's friends would just come in this way."

A set of stairs went down, and around the corner, the kitchen started. At least the corner that used to be there. Sam had commissioned a contractor to take down the wall concealing these stairs, and it felt like the house was twice as big with it gone. A stylish railing had been added, and the kitchen sat on one side of the stairs and the living room with his mother's upright piano sat on the other.

He whistled. "I haven't seen it like this."

"You haven't?"

"I've been having it remodeled. This is great." He moved to his left, which used to be blocked by another wall. He'd torn out all the carpet and replaced everything with a uniform laminate hardwood that could withstand snowy boots and muddy paws.

He ran his fingertips along the new windows and didn't feel the chill from outside. The paint on the wall reminded him of a watered down slate, and it brought a sense of peace to him.

"I hardly recognize this." Across the space, the kitchen cabinets had been stained a dark brown, and they made the space feel deeper and richer than before. Everything about this house now screamed high-end, and a rush of gratitude engulfed Sam. Gratitude that he had the money to remodel his parents' home into something they would be proud of.

"This is a beautiful house," Bonnie said, moving through the kitchen, touching the dining room table Sam had asked Rose-Marie to pick out for him. In fact, the owner of the furniture store in town had chosen everything on the main level.

A leather sofa and love seat waited in the living room, along with his mother's piano, an end table, and a lamp. Down the hall sat the master bedroom and bath, as well as the guest bath, and they should've been redone too.

Sam walked that way, babbling about the paint color he'd chosen and the reason he'd gone with quartz in the kitchen instead of granite. Bonnie trailed after him as he inspected the bathrooms and exclaimed over the new carpet in what would be his bedroom.

"Sorry," he said after a few minutes. "I just haven't seen the house in a few months. It's looking good, don't you think?" He finally focused on her, and a blip of discomfort pinged through him when he caught the gloomy look on her face. "What's wrong?" He ran his hands up her arms, glad the heat worked in the farmhouse.

"Sam," she said. "I was imagining this quaint little two-room house in the middle of a big piece of land." She leaned into him and he gathered her into his arms. She fit beside him, and he wanted her there all the time. Gazing down at her, he allowed himself to classify his feelings in that moment as love.

Sam loved Bonnie.

He'd known it for a while, but he hadn't dared admit it to himself, and he hadn't breathed a word of it to anyone else.

"But this…this is a castle. A farm-castle in the middle a big piece of land."

"I couldn't stomach the thought of leaving it as it was," he said in a quiet voice. "That was my parents' house, and it made me sad. But this—this is going to be *my* home, and I wanted to make it mine."

"Are you happy with it?"

"Yes," he said. "Do you like it?"

She stepped out of his arms and retreated down the hall. She rubbed her hands up her arms as if cold and said, "It's not my house. Doesn't matter if I like it."

But Sam really wanted her to like it. Really wanted her to live here with him, as his wife. He bit back the words and followed her into the living room. She wasn't ready to hear anything like what he had pulsing through his brain, and he couldn't order it into coherence anyway.

"Want me to drive you back to town now?" he asked, wondering if he'd made the right decision in bringing her out here to the farm.

She shook her head. "Not yet. Do you have any hot chocolate in this castle? Maybe some popcorn? Do the TVs work?" She looked around. "Do you even have a TV?"

He grinned at her, took her hand in his, and led her around the railing and into the kitchen. "I have hot chocolate and popcorn, and yes, there's a TV downstairs." He opened the fridge and promptly closed it. "We'll have to make the hot chocolate with water."

"Hmm," she said, a twinkle in her eye. "Sub-par, but I suppose it'll do." Her earlier melancholy seemed to have fled, and Sam wanted the rest of the evening to be picture-perfect. So he stuffed away his feelings, his wonderings, his questions, and focused on the fact that Bonnie was here. Bonnie had come.

Please let everything work out from here, he prayed as he mixed hot chocolate powder into mugs of boiling water.

Bonnie adored Coral Canyon, a fact which only added another pin to her heart. She could see herself living in that farmhouse, cooking dinner at the gas stove, and chopping onions on the quartz countertops.

She dreamt of such things, in fact. Dreamt of them in a lumpy hotel bed while he surely slept on a mattress of clouds and goose down in that fancy farmhouse at the base of the mountains.

The mountains! She'd never seen anything like them, and they called to her in a way nothing in Island Park ever had. Yes, Wyoming possessed a spirit Bonnie had been lacking, and she wondered for the hundredth time if she could leave her mother and move to Coral Canyon to be with Sam.

Bonnie thought of her mother as she waited in the lobby for Sam to arrive. Her mom had been doing okay, but Bonnie definitely detected some changes in her. She seemed thinner, though she ate. She felt ages older, though only a couple of months had passed since her husband's death.

For one brief, wild moment, Bonnie wondered if her mother could come to Coral Canyon too. Sam had that big ole farmhouse, with four bedrooms downstairs....

"Hey, beautiful." He arrived in front of her and swept a good morning kiss across her cheek. "You hungry?"

She stood and drank in the sight of him in his navy jeans and brown wool coat. He looked half country, half city, and she liked both sides of him. "Starved."

"Because we get a lot of tourists, there's plenty of places to eat," he said. "Are you feeling like traditional breakfast foods or something a little more adventurous?"

"Define 'adventurous'."

"Buffalo sausage. Elk steak and eggs."

She wrinkled her nose. She was country, but not quite that country. "Traditional."

He started toward the exit. "I've never been into the game meats either."

"No? Not even growing up here?"

"Not much of a hunter." He flashed her a smile as he held open her door. She paused inside his personal bubble and gave herself a moment to study him. Really look at him, right into his soul. A sense of warmth cascaded over her skin, and a feeling of rightness entered her mind. The sensation lasted for only a moment, and then she sank into the passenger seat.

Sam took an extra moment to close the door, and she

wondered if he'd felt the same thing as her. *What does it mean?* she wondered, but the Lord didn't answer. Sam started the car and pulled out of the hotel parking lot.

"Sam, I think I'm ready to answer one of your questions." Bonnie had been thinking about a lot of things over the past few weeks. Kids. Kids with Sam. Moving. Moving here to be with Sam. *Sam, Sam, Sam.*

He was everywhere, all the time. And Bonnie didn't seem to mind. Every time she went to bed at night, Sam entered her mind. She'd discovered she was happier now than she'd been since Jeff's death.

"Bonnie?" Sam asked, and she got the impression it wasn't the first time.

"I—I think I'd like to have more kids." She exhaled in a long sigh. "Being Jeff's mom was the best thing I ever was. I'd…like…another chance at that."

Sam's hand found hers, but Bonnie couldn't look at him. She hadn't really examined how much of a failure she'd been. How much she blamed herself for Jeff's death.

Sam pulled into another parking lot and faced her. "Thank you for telling me, Bonnie." He seemed to see right past all her insecurities, all her weaknesses, and she liked that he gazed at her with such adoration despite her flaws. He almost made her feel worthy of his affection.

He cradled her face in his palm and kissed her. She returned his kiss, stroke for stroke, and she wondered how on earth she could give him up, let him walk out of her life, allow him to move to this charming town without her.

———

THE FLIGHT HOME WAS SATURATED WITH GREEN. BONNIE herself had packed a green sweater, but Sam hadn't brought one green thing. He'd seemed quite disgruntled about that fact too, though Bonnie couldn't figure out why.

"I just pay attention to all the holidays because of my job," she'd told him. "Kids make a national event out of everything."

That had seemed to cheer him, and he'd fallen asleep on the plane. She watched him without shame since he couldn't see her. She loved the lines of his face, the soft way his chest rose and fell, the absolute joy she experienced from being with him.

Gently, so she wouldn't wake him, she reached over and slipped her fingers into his. He didn't stir, and she relaxed back into the seat and closed her eyes too. She imagined herself living in that luxury farmhouse, and it wasn't that hard. Sure, she'd miss her friends. A pang of sadness pulled through her at not being able to confide in Michelle in the mornings and running into Cheryl at The Juice Bar.

She'd miss her mother, and all the kids at school, and everything she'd built for herself in Island Park, even if it was only a small house with a big dog inside.

And if she were being honest, and twenty-thousand feet up, with nothing else to do and so close to the heavens, she figured she might as well be honest with herself— she wondered if she could truly leave Jeff in Island Park.

Paul didn't seem to have a problem not being in town. Bonnie wondered if he thought about their son, if he lost any sleep over their failed marriage. *Of course he does*, she thought. Paul wasn't a monster. He'd lost a son and a wife too.

A fountain of forgiveness washed over her, a feeling she hadn't expected. She hadn't truly realized that she hadn't forgiven Paul, but with her hand in Sam's and her heart wide open, she let herself feel the cleansing power of forgiveness.

A single tear escaped her left eye, and she was glad it was on the opposite side from Sam. She reached up and brushed it away, hoping that the next ten weeks with him would be nothing but wonderful.

———

"I AM IN REAL TROUBLE," SHE ANNOUNCED THE NEXT morning. Michelle looked up and sprang from her desk.

"How was the trip? Did you like Coral Canyon? Is the house nice?" She reached Bonnie and embraced her, stepping back and holding onto her shoulders. "Did Sam propose on the front porch?"

Bonnie trilled out a laugh and shook her head, her hair swishing around her face. "No. Now anything I say is going to sound lame."

"No, it's not. Tell me." The eagerness in Michelle's eyes testified that the single-and-searching event over Valentine's Day hadn't resulted in anyone for her.

"The town is wonderful." Bonnie sighed as she sank into the chair behind the horseshoe-shaped table where she did the reading groups. "The house is newly remodeled with hardwood and quartz and slate-gray paint. Sam is as perfect as ever." Something Bonnie could only identify as bliss traveled through her.

"And I'm in real trouble."

"Why's that?"

"He leaves in ten weeks."

"Maybe you'll go with him."

Bonnie shook her head. "And do what? Live where?"

Michelle waved her hand like such details would work themselves out. "Sometimes you just need to take that first leap of faith."

"I can't go with him if we're not married, and we're not going to get married in less than ten weeks."

"Why not?"

Michelle looked serious too, and Bonnie sputtered, unable to come up with a proper explanation beyond, "Ten weeks, Michelle."

"What do you need to get married?" she challenged, even putting her hands on her hips. She looked very stern-teacher when she did, and Bonnie wilted a little. "A dress? I'll buy you that. Some flowers? Let's go down to Allie right now."

"We can't go right now," Bonnie said, half-amused and half-disgusted.

"Why not?" Michelle asked again.

The bell rang, and Bonnie stood up. "School's starting, that's why not."

Michelle normally went to get the kids from the playground right when the bell rang, but she kept her gaze burning into Bonnie's for a few extra moments. "Details," she said again before spinning on her heel and clicking out of the classroom and down the hall.

Bonnie collapsed back into the chair, her mind spinning through the dozens and dozens of details that would need to be worked out in just ten short weeks.

The first was whether or not she wanted to marry Sam Buttars.

The second was whether or not she'd really go with him to Wyoming.

"Two *major* details," she muttered to herself as she pulled the clipboard toward her. She hadn't been at work yet this week, and she had no idea what to start with that morning.

By the grace of God, she made it through the day. Avoided Michelle's questions and daggered glares. Arrived at home to the welcome sight of Boyfriend and his slobber stain on her couch. When she and Sam had returned to Steeple Ridge yesterday, Logan had joked that he was thinking about keeping Boyfriend for himself.

"Of course, I'd have to rename him," he'd said. "Do you think he'd mind if I called him Girlfriend?"

Bonnie had laughed, but she'd also seen and heard the loneliness in Logan's voice and on his face. Her heart ached for him—for the whole farmhouse full of single men out at Steeple Ridge.

She'd prayed for all of them last night, pouring her heart out to God that He would lead them toward their future of happiness.

The next time she saw Sam, he wore a tie with his

cowboy hat, and he appeared at the end of her row with the words, "Is this seat taken?"

She jumped to her feet, nearly twisting her ankle in the process. Her gaze flew to the back right corner of the chapel, where Sam usually sat with his brothers. Darren sat on the end of the pew now, no room for Sam at all.

"You want to sit by me?" She didn't mean for her voice to come out so squeaky or so high.

Sam's neck turned the color of cooked beets, and the sound of his boots on the floor scraped through the room. Embarrassment heated her own face, and she made a clunking sound as her back hit the bench when she tried to sit.

He slid onto the seat beside her, as graceful as always. She felt like a dwarf next to him, and she'd never felt like that before. The low chatter in the chapel seemed to have died, as if everyone was so occupied with staring at the two of them.

Sam lifted his arm and put it around her, pulling her into his side. "I should've talked to you about this," he said.

"I don't mind," she whispered back. Safe within the strength of his embrace, Bonnie suddenly didn't care what anyone thought. If anyone was looking. A sense of possessiveness came over her, and she raised her chin in a defiant gesture. Everyone *should* know Sam Buttars was with her.

Pastor Gray stood up and started his sermon. Halfway through the lesson on the Savior as the Great Mediator, Bonnie realized her mom hadn't come in. Immediate worry wormed through her, and she started scanning the few rows she could see to find her mom. They'd been sitting together since Paul's departure, but Bonnie couldn't find her.

Sam leaned down and practically grazed her earlobe when he asked, "You okay?"

"My mom didn't come in, did she?"

Sam wasn't nearly as discreet as Bonnie, and he swiveled his head in each direction a couple of times before saying, "I don't see her."

"We should go visit her after choir practice."

He nodded and squeezed her shoulder. Bonnie tried to refocus on the sermon, but she couldn't. Her mind whirred through why her mother hadn't come to church. Bonnie had only been over to see her once this week, and she'd spent the whole time talking about Coral Canyon and Sam.

Guilt gutted her. She hadn't even noticed how her mother was doing during the visit. She'd been so wrapped up in herself. Was that how she'd been while her son drowned? So engaged in her own friendship and conversation that she hadn't even noticed where her own flesh and blood was?

Her eyes burned, burned. She couldn't hold back the tears. A sob gathered in her throat, choking her. Images flashed through her mind.

Blue sky.

Green grass.

Baseball fields.

Black jogging path.

Yellow flowers.

Football coach gesturing.

Kids running on the playground.

Murky pond water.

Gray T-shirt.

Jeff face-down.

Bonnie's legs felt as soaked now as they did that autumn day she'd ran into the pond, nearly gone under herself in her haste to get to her son.

"Bonnie, come on." Sam spoke right out loud, and she couldn't resist the pressure against her hand. He lifted her into his arms, and it was in that moment that she realized someone was crying. Wailing, actually.

It wasn't until Darren and Logan and Ben met Sam at the back door of the chapel with worried expressions that she realized the sound was coming from her throat.

CHAPTER
SIXTEEN

Sam had no idea what to do to help Bonnie. His brothers flanked him, and that alone kept him moving toward the truck. "Darren," he said, and the next oldest Buttars took an extra-long step and appeared at Sam's side.

"Call her mom," he said. "She was worried about her."

"All right." He didn't ask how to get the number. Darren would figure it out, the way he always did.

"Logan," Sam said.

"Right here."

"Go get Boyfriend." He unlooped Bonnie's purse from her arm, which hung at her side, lifeless. "Take her car. It's a blue sporty thing. She lives over on Pheasant Road. White house. Third one down on the left."

"Got it." Again, Logan could problem-solve to get an address, as he'd never been to Bonnie's.

"Ben, can you and Rae help me get her calmed down

and out to the farm? Maybe find her friend, Michelle." Sam's fight or flight instinct fired on all cylinders, and he managed to get the truck door open while Ben went jogging back toward the church.

"Bonnie," Sam said in a soft but firm voice. "Are you with me, sweetheart?" She'd stopped crying—the sound had actually started as a low shriek in the back of her throat. It had grown no matter what he'd said to her, and he'd realized pretty quick that she couldn't even hear him.

She seemed catatonic now. Her eyes were open, but she stared at nothing. Sam wondered if he should take her to the emergency room.

"Her mom is fine," Darren said. "She's on the phone, and wants to talk to Bonnie."

"Did you hear that, love? We've got your mom on the phone. She's just fine."

Sam nodded to Darren, who said, "Here she is, ma'am," and held the phone to Bonnie's ear. Warblings came through the line, but Sam's adrenaline pulsed and his own heartbeat banged loudly in his ears.

He met Darren's eye and wasn't comforted by the extreme worry there. It was the same look his brother had worn when Sam had shown up in Coral Canyon and told them they were leaving after the funeral.

Darren put the phone back to his ear. "No, ma'am… Yes, I understand." He pulled the phone back from his mouth. "She said to take her to the hospital."

Determined, Sam nodded. But Ben and Rae—along with Missy and Tucker and Michelle and another woman Sam felt like he should know—arrived.

Voices spoke, but Sam didn't know what to do. Who to listen to. All he could see was his beautiful Bonnie in absolute agony. She sat behind the wheel of his truck, seemingly without a bone in her body.

"Bonnie," he whispered, leaning into the truck and placing a kiss right behind her ear. "I love you. Please, please, come back to me." His voice faded into nothing on the last word, but Bonnie didn't respond.

Sam couldn't fall apart now. He wouldn't. "I'm going to take her to the hospital. Ben, call Logan and tell him to forget about Boyfriend." Sam lifted Bonnie into his arms again. "Someone help me get that other door open?"

He wasn't even sure who did it, but the door was open when he arrived on the other side of the truck, and he carefully laid Bonnie on the passenger side of the bench seat. He hurried around to the driver's side and paused when he saw the sea of faces that had gathered.

Not just Bonnie's friends and his brothers. But the entire church congregation had come out, Pastor Gray right there at the front. Sam pulled his hat down so no one would see him cry, and then he decided he didn't care if they did.

"I'll keep everyone updated," he said, unsure of how he'd even do that. He had the phone numbers of five people standing in front of him. But he trusted in the networking skills of the town. He trusted the townspeople would be praying.

He trusted God.

And with that faith firmly in place, he climbed into the

truck, a constant prayer in the back of his throat and the front of his mind as he drove.

———

AN HOUR LATER, SAM RETURNED TO THE WAITING ROOM FROM his pacing down the hall to find Darren looking around. "Hey." Sam approached him. "What are you doin' here?"

"I came to sit with you." He claimed a chair, leaving Sam little choice but to sit next to him.

"You didn't need to come."

Darren said, "Have you heard anything?"

Sam exhaled. "Nothing yet. They took her back and last time I asked, the receptionist said she'd have a doctor come talk to me." Frustration roared through him, making his stomach sour.

"What happened? Do you know?"

"I have no idea," Sam said. "She asked if I'd seen her mother. I said no. She seemed okay. Suggested we go visit her after choir practice." Sam thought back, trying to sort through what had happened during church. "Then she just sort of started…moaning. Then it escalated." Sam couldn't get the shriek out of his ears. The horrible, high-pitched sound had attached itself to his soul.

"What are you gonna do now?"

"I have no idea."

"When are you gonna tell her you love her? She'd go to Coral Canyon if you told her."

Thankfully, Sam was saved from answering by a nurse who called, "Bonnie Sherman?"

He shot to his feet and strode toward her. "I'm with Bonnie Sherman."

"She's asking for Sam Buttars."

"I'm Sam Buttars."

The nurse turned and went through a door, leaving Sam to follow. Only thirty seconds later, she showed him into a narrow room with a narrow bed where Bonnie lay. Her cheeks held a healthy blush, which sent relief through Sam.

"Hey, sweetheart." He took her hand into both of his and pressed a kiss to her forehead. "How are you feeling?"

She didn't answer for several long moments, her throat working as she blinked back tears. "Confused," she finally said. "The doctor said I had a panic attack."

"In church," Sam confirmed. "I carried you out and brought you here." He stroked his thumb down the side of her hand. "Do you remember that?"

She turned her head, which caused her tears to streak her cheek on that side of her face. "No."

"Were you worried about your mom? We called her. She's okay. She told Darren she just didn't feel like leaving the house today."

Bonnie nodded, her chin trembling. Sam's lungs pinched. His heart twisted. He'd do almost anything to take this pain from her.

"Tell me what to do," he begged, his voice overflowing with emotion.

She wouldn't look at him, but she said, "I want to go home."

"Let me go find the nurse." Sam lifted her hand to his

lips and pressed a kiss to her wrist. "I—I'll go find the nurse." He made a hasty exit, completely baffled as to why he thought now would be a good time to tell her he loved her.

Because it so wasn't.

He found a nurse sitting at a desk and asked about Bonnie. She said she'd go find her chart and be right back. "Be right back" to a nurse must mean "sixteen minutes later," because that was when she returned.

"The doctor wants to check her one more time, and he wants her to schedule an appointment with the hospital psychologist. Then she can go."

Sam nodded, his jaw tight. "How long?"

"He's in with her now."

He thanked her and walked slowly back to Bonnie's room. The doctor slipped out as Sam rounded the corner, and he paused. "Are you with Bonnie?" the doctor asked.

"Yes."

"She shouldn't be alone."

"I can stay with her and take her to her mother's after that." Sam really wanted to take her back to Steeple Ridge and never let her out of his sight again. He wanted to wake up next to her. Go to sleep with her curled into his side. Lounge around in his pajamas while she made coffee. Serve her breakfast in bed on Mother's Day.

"She has an appointment tomorrow at ten o'clock. She's on a pretty significant dosage of medication that will make her tired. She shouldn't drive."

"I'll take care of her," Sam said, and it almost sounded like a vow.

The doctor smiled, but it didn't hold much happiness, and nodded before he left Sam standing in the hallway alone.

Sam's own anxiety threatened to crush him, but he put on a brave face before entering Bonnie's room. He found her sitting on the bed with her arms clenched across her chest.

"Hey, love. You ready?"

She swung her attention toward him, her head almost wobbling on her neck. "Yeah." Her speech wasn't exactly slow, but she didn't seem as awake as she had been.

"Let's go." Sam held onto her elbow as they walked down the hall and out into the waiting room. Darren met them with affection on his face. In that moment, Sam realized how much Bonnie meant to all of them, and a rush of gratitude for such a strong family bond soared through him.

"I brought her car," he said. "I'll just follow you back to her place and then take the truck home."

"That's fine," Sam said.

"Fine," Bonnie echoed, and Sam started praying again.

———

SHE SLEPT MOST OF THE AFTERNOON, A DEEP SLEEP THAT MADE Sam envious. He caught a few winks here and there, but he couldn't turn off his mind. Logan had taken Boyfriend anyway, and the house was calm and quiet.

Sam set a pair of bread slices in the toaster and wandered down the hall to Bonnie's den. He wasn't sure why, only that he wanted to feel closer to her and he thought the best place for that was with her piano.

He sat on the bench and ran his fingers across the keys without pressing them and making music. The unique scent of Bonnie's perfume lingered in the air, along with a hint of sugared lemon. He found the source of that in a half-burned yellow candle on the end table next to the couch.

Right next to that, he lifted a picture frame holding a portrait of a little boy. He recognized Bonnie's beautiful strawberry-kissed hair, her heart-shaped face. Jeff grinned like it was Christmas morning, and for all Sam knew, it could've been.

He didn't know what her first husband looked like, but Sam knew that if he and Bonnie were to have a child, her fairer features would get overshadowed by his darker ones. He tried to picture Jeff with dark hair and chocolatey eyes, but he couldn't. The little boy was angelic exactly as he was.

He reset the picture on the table and sighed. The faint smell of browned bread reached him, and he hurried out of this space that was the epitome of Bonnie, more hopeful than he'd been since she'd started weeping that morning.

He hummed to himself and started opening her cupboards. He'd stay as late as he could stand, and then he'd deliver her to her mother. Michelle had already texted to say she'd taken care of work for a couple of days, and Sam had spent a large percentage of time updating his brothers and Tucker and the pastor.

He'd put together quite a good pot of spaghetti and

meatballs when she finally stirred. He went straight to her side but didn't touch her.

She moaned, but it wasn't the awful, low sound of hysteria. "My head hurts."

"I made dinner," he said. "I'll bring you something to drink and some painkillers." When he returned to her side after rifling through a cabinet in her bathroom to find the ibuprofen, she'd tucked herself into a seated position in the corner of the couch.

She smiled up at him with all the charm she always had and swallowed the pills. "I'm really sorry about today," she said.

"Nothing to be sorry about." He went into the kitchen. "Want something to eat?"

"Yes, I'm starving."

He served up two bowls of spaghetti and handed her one. As the stress of the day wound down and Sam realized that Bonnie wasn't all the way broken—maybe just bruised—his exhaustion swept over him.

"I let my memories of that day out," she said once both of their empty bowls rested on the coffee table. "Even on the anniversary of Jeff's death, I don't let myself go back to that park."

"Have you ever been back? Physically, I mean."

"No."

Sam wasn't sure what he would do if he were in her position. He didn't know exactly where his parents' plane had gone down. He hadn't been there to witness the deaths. He didn't have to avoid certain streets to contain horrific memories.

"Let's go for a walk." Bonnie pushed herself off the couch and took the dishes into the kitchen. Sam didn't particularly want to go for a walk, but he wanted to be with Bonnie, so he put on his coat, glad his gloves were in the pockets, and stepped into the darkness with her.

A week later, Bonnie seemed to be back to her regular self. She'd gone to work the last half of the week. She'd sat by him at church without incident. Her fingers were flawless on the piano keys during choir practice. Her lips were perfectly glossed; not a hair sat out of place; Sam loved her, strengths and weaknesses and everything in between.

She came out to the farm, the way she usually did on Sunday afternoons. They rode horses and talked with his brothers and ate the dinner Missy and Tucker brought. Sam still hadn't breathed a word of his feelings to her. She hadn't regressed, exactly, but something inside him whispered that she needed more time.

Unfortunately, time was literally the one thing Sam was running short of.

Sometime in the middle of the night, his phone rang. He startled and sat straight up in bed, his heart pounding. His phone went to Do Not Disturb at ten o'clock every night. If it was ringing, the same number had called twice within two minutes.

He fumbled for the flashing screen and swiped on the call while his mind registered the name Westin Stone—his neighbor in Wyoming.

"Hello?" Sam said.

"Sam, it's Westin. I know it's late there."

Sam switched on the lamp and swung his legs over the

edge of the bed, dread making his stomach heavy. "What's going on?"

"I don't know why, but I had a feeling I needed to go check on the farmhouse. I'm glad I did, because I managed to get the water turned off and the pump in the basement started."

Sam's blood raced. "Water?"

"It's been really warm here all week. Rained a lot too. We're flooding all over the place."

Sam stood as if he'd leave for Wyoming right now. "My house is flooded?"

"I'm afraid so. We've got the sump pump going now, and I'm having Leroy go over in the morning and put another one on a cycle, so the first doesn't burn out."

"I'll be there tomorrow," Sam said, fully awake now and already pulling a suitcase from his closet. He knew very little about sump pumps—only that they pumped groundwater away from the house—but he knew "flooding" meant "bad." Especially in a house with brand new flooring and paint.

He wasn't entirely sure what he could do, but he wanted to be there to make decisions. He was sure Westin would need money to keep his house dry. And so he packed, got on the Internet and bought a ticket for the next flight out of New York, and went to wake up Darren.

CHAPTER
SEVENTEEN

When she woke, Bonnie's phone flashed with blue and green lights. Green meant Facebook message, which meant someone who didn't have Bonnie's phone number, which most likely meant someone Bonnie didn't want to talk to.

Blue meant text messages, and she swiped on the phone to check them. Michelle, her mom, Cheryl. Bonnie didn't have time to read them all right now. Already overwhelmed, and only Monday, she put the phone face-down on the nightstand and went to get ready for work.

By the time she got to school, she was ready to go home again. She'd taken so much time off work, though, that she couldn't leave. So she summoned as much patience and energy as she could and entered the classroom.

Michelle met her eye from the front of the room, where she'd already gathered the students for their Monday meeting. Bonnie hadn't realized she hadn't even beaten the morning bell, and she slunk to her seat, putting her lunch and purse on the floor behind her instead of in Michelle's closet the way she normally did.

She pulled her reading groups folder toward her and opened it, determined not to let Monday get the better of her. She made it through her groups, took one of the students down to their special education class, and made it back to the room just as Michelle started a movie.

Bonnie thought that odd, as Michelle usually reserved movies for Friday afternoons. Sure enough, Michelle said, "Boys and girls, I'll be right back." She met Bonnie's eye, latched onto her elbow, and towed her back into the hall. "Have you even looked at your phone today?"

Bonnie's heart rate spiked. "I did this morning, for a minute."

"Sam's gone to Wyoming. His house flooded."

Her concern intensified. "All right," she said. "Is he hurt?"

"No."

"Are any of his brothers hurt?"

"No."

Bonnie cocked her head, surprised at how calm she was. "So it's only the house."

The intensity in Michelle's gaze didn't lessen. "He wants you to call him."

"He's talking to you?"

"Because you won't answer your messages."

"Should I do it now?"

"Yes. Go get your phone and let him know you're okay."

Bonnie complied, the hint of a headache starting behind her right eye. Her phone flashed brilliantly, and she didn't even see Sam's name on the notifications on the home screen. She had too many texts to see his, so she swiped the phone open and went to her texting app. Sure enough, he'd texted eleven times.

I know it's early, and you probably won't be awake for a while.

My house in Wyoming flooded and I'm on a plane right now. We're taking off in fifteen minutes and I won't have service for a few hours.

I'll call you when I get there.

I'm here now. The whole basement is wet. My neighbor got a pump going last night, but its not working fast enough.

Going to get another pump.

Everything is installed. We have the pumps cycling every nineteen minutes so one doesn't overheat. Now all I can do is wait. And try to dry out the flooring.

I'm going to breakfast at Margie's, and I wish you were here with me.

I was gone less than an hour, and when I came home the power was off at the house. Which means the pumps weren't working. Which means the basement is filling with water again.

There's SO MUCH water here. Groundwater, and rain water, and all the melting snow...

Westin says I need new pumps. They blew the circuit in the house. That's why the power was out. It's been an hour and there is literally water everywhere. I think I'm going to be here for a few weeks taking care of this.

Can you call me when you get a minute?

Bonnie glanced up from her phone, her emotions spiraling from the way he missed her to the fact that he wasn't coming right back to Island Park. She lifted the phone to her ear, and the automatic call mode enabled.

Sam answered on the first ring. "Bonnie," he said.

"I'm so sorry about your house. How's it going?"

He exhaled and she imagined him scrubbing his hand through the hair on the back of his neck, the way he did when he was thinking or frustrated. "Still installing the first new pump. The water's to the bottom step now. About six inches deep."

"Six inches?" Horror snaked through Bonnie. The farmhouse wasn't small by any means, even in the basement. And the whole bottom floor was covered in six inches of water? "You really will be there for a few weeks."

"Yeah."

Their phone conversations were much more awkward than their in-person ones. In his truck, she could let him drive for a few blocks until he was ready to speak. Now, only silence came through the line.

"What are you thinking?" she asked.

"I'm thinking I'm going to miss the Easter program."

"Oh." Bonnie hadn't even thought of that. Sure, she'd played for the choir the previous day, but once it was done, she didn't give it any more mental energy. She currently had a lot more to consider, but she realized Sam stewed on the Easter program a lot more than she did. As he should.

"Do you think if I asked Michelle, she could take over for me?"

"It's two weeks away," Bonnie said. "You don't think you'll be back by then?"

"It's impossible to know, and we have a rehearsal this Wednesday evening I'll miss for sure. And I won't be back by Sunday, I'm sure."

"Yeah, ask Michelle."

"I'd have you do it, but…." He let the sentence hang there, and Bonnie again disliked this phone conversation. In person, she'd be able to see his eyes, read his body language. He'd driven her to her psychologist appointment last Monday, and she had another one this afternoon. The hospital had said she needed to do four sessions before they'd close her case.

"I'm feeling much better," she told Sam, as if he'd asked. "I could do it, but it would be nice to have Michelle there too. She's a good music leader."

"I'll ask her."

"What else do you need me to do?" Her therapist had suggested finding ways to serve those around her as a way of getting outside of her own problems, but Bonnie hadn't quite taken the first step toward that yet.

"Nothing."

"Are you sure?"

"Maybe just call me again tonight? I like the sound of your voice."

Bonnie smiled and leaned into the brick wall. "I can do that."

"Are you really feeling better?"

"A lot better," she said. "Almost normal." Maybe she could cancel her appointment that afternoon. But somewhere deep inside her mind, something whispered that she absolutely shouldn't cancel. That she needed the extra help at this point in her life.

Michelle opened the door, and Bonnie said, "I have to go, Sam. I—I'll call you tonight."

"All right," he said. "Bye, Bonnie. Love you."

Bonnie was about to say good-bye but sucked back the word. "Love you?" she whispered. The line was dead; Sam was gone; Michelle waited only ten feet down the hall. Bonnie pulled the phone from her ear and stared at it.

Did Sam Buttars love her?

Michelle approached as if Bonnie were a frightened cat. "What's wrong?"

"He just said, 'Love you.'" Bonnie looked at her friend, pure adrenaline and awe pulling through her. "Do you think he meant that?"

Michelle's worry softened, and so did the lines around her face. "Yes, Bonnie, I think he probably did. Have you even seen the way Sam looks at you?"

"Of course I have."

Michelle shook her head. "I don't think so. If you'd really *seen* the way he looks at you, you'd already know he's in love with you." She grinned and gently took the phone from Bonnie's nearly limp fingers. "Now, I'm sure he's kicking himself really hard about now. He'll have a big explanation ready for next time he talks to you."

"You think so?"

"He won't want that to be the way he tells you he loves you." The bell rang, startling Michelle. "Recess." She returned to the classroom, the children spilling from it a few moments later. The whole hallway filled with kids on their way outside. They flowed around Bonnie like a fast-moving river. She didn't move, could hardly breathe.

Sam was in love with her.

A smile finally broke through the trance she'd fallen into, and she bounced back into the classroom to hash out her next steps with Michelle.

―――――

Days turned into a week. Bonnie was exceedingly glad she had Boyfriend, as her real boyfriend hadn't come home from Wyoming yet. She called him each evening before she went to bed, staying up as late as she dared. With Sam two hours behind her, the system was working.

Except that, for Bonnie, it wasn't. She'd hung up with him thirty minutes ago and still couldn't fall asleep.

"This is what your life will be like when he moves permanently," she said to the dark room. The mattress shifted as Boyfriend lifted his head.

She didn't want this kind of relationship. One where she imagined what Sam wore, and what his facial expressions were as he said certain things. One where she spoke to him only over a line and never got to hold his hand or kiss him.

And church yesterday had been an absolute mess. Without Sam by her side, she felt lost, adrift in a sea of townspeople she'd spent years isolating herself from. None of them acted like it though. She still had a freezer full of food from her episode two weeks ago, and the woman in charge of service groups at the church was still sending people once a week with cards, flowers, conversation, and food.

The next morning, Bonnie arrived at the hospital a few minutes early. Her principal had been nothing but kind about the time off Bonnie needed, and she found that she felt loads better after her sessions with Dr. Huff.

"You ready, Bonnie?" The doctor herself stood in the doorway, smiling to reveal her perfectly straight teeth.

Bonnie liked her a lot, and she stood and followed her back into her office. "I like your skirt."

Dr. Huff beamed back at her. "Thank you. I made it myself." She swished the fabric with her hand.

"You did? Wow." Bonnie sat in the comfortable recliner. "I can't even sew a straight line."

"You could do this. It's a simple pattern."

Bonnie just smiled. She hadn't lied when she'd said she couldn't sew. The pillowcase she'd attempted in high school testified of her non-abilities with a sewing machine. Not that she'd tried since, but she was okay with some of her weaknesses.

"Tell me how your week was."

"Not bad," Bonnie said, the words mostly true. The week hadn't been good, but it hadn't been bad either. What sat between the two? She didn't know, but she added, "I talked to Sam every night. His house is still under about an inch of water. He doesn't think he's going to make it back in time for the Easter program." Bonnie's voice shook and she didn't even know where the emotion had come from. It was just suddenly there, infusing her voice and making her chin tremble.

"How do you feel about that?"

"Not good," Bonnie said, letting a tear slide down her face. Maybe being able to cry without embarrassment was more therapeutic than she'd originally thought. "I miss him."

"I'm sure he misses you too."

"I'm scared he's never going to come back."

"Has he said that?"

"No." Bonnie wiped her face. "But he was planning to move there permanently at the end of May, and that's only seven weeks from now. If I were him, I'd just stay there."

Dr. Huff let several seconds of silence go by. "What will you do when he moves there permanently?"

"I don't know."

"Has he asked you to go with him?"

Bonnie lifted one shoulder. "Sort of?"

"He *sort of* asked you to move fifteen hundred miles?" The incredulity in Dr. Huff's voice screamed through the room.

"I went to visit with him a month or so ago. It is a beautiful town."

"What would it take for you to move there?"

Love you.

Sam had never brought up those two words, and everything in Bonnie had morphed into a chicken when she called him. He hadn't said them again, though, which led her to believe he knew he had.

"I don't know," Bonnie finally said.

"Something to think about," Dr. Huff said, the same way Sam always had. The easy acceptance of her indecision and truly not knowing how she felt or what she should do was so cleansing.

It was one of the things she loved most about Sam.

Loved?

Bonnie stood and managed to pay for her appointment, make another one, and escape the office without having to examine her feelings further.

She sat in the car, utterly exhausted. She'd had no idea that thinking could take so much energy.

"Maybe all you need is love," she said to herself as she drove from the hospital to the elementary school. "Maybe The Beatles got it right."

Bonnie certainly didn't know, and she parked, pulled out her phone, and thumbed out *Miss you* to Sam before going in to work.

Miss you too came back right as she entered the building.

CHAPTER
EIGHTEEN

Sam did not know this much water existed on the Earth. Wasn't ninety percent of it supposed to be contained in the oceans?

He figured he had the other ten percent in his base-ment. Still. The stripe on his credit card was starting to malfunction he'd run it so many times in that ratty old reader at the hardware store. He hadn't been able to buy dinner last night with that card, and it wasn't because he didn't have money.

He expected Bonnie's call in the next several minutes, as she'd been calling close to eight o'clock every night. The sun had shone all day, but Sam wasn't sure if he should be glad about that or worried that even more snow had melted in the mountains.

"I love you," Sam practiced as he put a frying pan on the stove. Westin's wife had brought him a plastic container of chicken cordon bleu and wild rice at four o'clock, but he was hungry again. With the amount of work he put into every day, it was no wonder.

He had the butter hot and two eggs cracked in the pan when his phone rang. "Hey, beautiful," he said after connecting the call.

"Hey, yourself." Bonnie sounded jovial, upbeat. The simple cadence of her voice was like music to his ears, and she seemed to be improving with every day that passed. "How's the house?"

He'd grown tired of updating everyone. Between Ben and Tucker and Bonnie, he'd taken to saying, "It's a house. I'll fix it up." He took a deep breath, the words he'd known he needed to say surging forward. "Bonnie, I'm not going to make it home for the Easter performance."

"Like, at all?"

"Like at all."

"Oh."

He hated the wounded quality of her voice, but he couldn't help it. He'd need to be on a plane by Saturday morning to make it back in time, with any semblance of being human, and he just couldn't imagine a scenario where his basement was water-free that quickly.

At first, he'd thought it would be a quick fix. Get out here, put in a new pump, voila. Water gone.

But that hadn't happened, and Sam didn't know what to do about it. He hadn't brought more than a couple days' worth of clothes, which had forced him to buy new items in town. He didn't need to go back to Island Park for much. A few more clothes and personal items. His horse.

Bonnie.

"Could you record the program for me?" he asked.

"Sure."

She didn't say anything else, and Sam's exhaustion prevented his brain from coming up with anything suitable to discuss.

Love you.

He wasn't going to bring that up. He wasn't.

She hadn't, and he half-hoped she hadn't heard him.

"Sam?"

"Yeah?"

"Are you going to come back to Island Park at all?"

Sam didn't think. No one had asked him that, but the answer was right there in the back of his throat. He forced it out. "No."

A quick, tight sound came through the line. Could've been a gasp. Or a sigh. Or an inhalation.

"I'm sorry, Bonnie," he said, the words flowing easily now. "I didn't know this was going to happen. But I'd be leaving in a few weeks anyway, and I don't really have a lot out there. Darren could probably pack it all up and mail it to me. And I've got this huge problem here, and I think…I think I'm just going to stay."

For a moment, Sam felt like he was falling, the sensation unwelcome and unpleasant. His fingers hurt from how hard he gripped the phone, but he didn't dare release them for fear of dropping the device, missing Bonnie's reaction.

She didn't give one, which only added pain to Sam's guilt. "I'm sorry, Bonnie." He couldn't quite get himself to invite her to come to Coral Canyon. Or to tell her he loved her. Neither item would help. She couldn't leave her job in Island Park at the beginning of April, and she was nowhere near ready to repeat "I love you" back to him. He wouldn't leave that bombshell out there. Didn't want to be around when it exploded.

The scent of burning butter and egg met his nose, and Sam lunged for the frying pan on the stove. He removed it, the sound of metal on metal almost unbearable as he tossed the pan away from the heat.

She finally said, "I understand, Sam."

But he didn't think she did. *He* barely understood.

"Are you going to get yourself a dog?" she asked.

"Yeah," he said, staring at his ruined dinner.

"What kind?"

Sam couldn't believe this was what they were talking about. A dog? Didn't she want to know if she could join him in Wyoming? Could they date long-distance? Sam hadn't been too great at dating short-distance, and the thought of weekend trips and daily phone calls constituting a relationship didn't appeal to him.

"So there's this breed Logan's been telling me about," Sam said. "A poodle and an Australian shepherd, which of course, Rambo is. It's called an Aussiedoodle."

"Oh, right," Bonnie said like she knew about the designer breed.

"Logan's looking around for me."

"From Island Park?"

"We use the Internet," Sam said, a teasing quality coming into his voice. "He can search as if he lived here."

"Of course." She exhaled and murmured something not meant for him. "Well, I have to go, Sam."

"Right." He didn't know how to end this conversation. Was this a final good-bye? Or like the others he'd experienced since he'd left in the dead of night?

"I probably won't call tomorrow," Bonnie said, her voice pitching up on the last word. "I think this is probably good-bye."

"It doesn't have to be."

"You're not coming back."

Sam stared out the window above the kitchen sink, the darkness out in the country something he'd always appreciated. "Maybe you could come here."

"I've thought about it."

Sam's pulse jumped. "And?"

"I don't know."

Sam nodded though she wasn't there and couldn't see him. "I'll be home in the fall for Ben's wedding."

"The wedding, right."

"What are you doin' this summer? Maybe you could—"

"I really have to go." So many emotions came with the words that Sam couldn't identify them all.

"Oh, all right, I'll talk to you later then." Sam waited for her to respond, but his phone beeped, indicating that the call had ended. He let his hand drop to his side, a white-hot knife of pain moving through his ribs and into his back.

He wasn't sure how long he stared out the window.

The darkness couldn't get any darker. He finally lifted his phone and texted Ben.

I think I just broke up with Bonnie.

His brother called not ten seconds later, but Sam didn't want to talk so he didn't answer. Instead he texted *Call me in the morning, okay? I need time to think.*

Don't think too hard, Ben sent back.

I'm not coming back to Island Park. Sam left the over-fried eggs on the stove and went down the hall to his bedroom.

Oh.

That was all Ben sent. *Oh.*

Bonnie had said the same thing when she'd learned he wouldn't be back in time for the Easter program. Ben didn't text again, a fact which made Sam grateful. Though it wasn't very late, he felt like he'd been carrying the weight of the world and he fell asleep with haunting images of a child with dark hair and eyes, a smattering of freckles across the bridge of her nose, and very pale skin on her heart-shaped face.

———

SAM HAD NOT BEEN TO CHURCH IN CORAL CANYON SINCE HIS arrival. It had only been one Sunday, and he'd spent it wearing rubber galoshes and a frown. He didn't feel much like going on Easter either, because he'd rather be in Vermont, nervous yet excited for the choir to put on their program.

He wondered if Bonnie would record it for him the way she'd said she would. She hadn't called on

Wednesday night. Nor Thursday, Friday, or Saturday. He couldn't bring himself to call her, though he had texted a couple of times.

I miss you.

And *Have you thought any more about coming out here?*

He'd only sent the first message, and Bonnie hadn't answered. He knew it was unfair of him—probably insensitive too—to say such things to her. He'd told her he wasn't coming back to Island Park.

He'd also told her he loved her. Asked her to come be where he was.

Anger surged, and Sam decided he really needed to go to church that morning, if only to find some peace for himself. Showered and dressed in a new green paisley tie and a suit he'd ordered from the department store in town, he set out in the new truck he'd purchased last week. After all, he couldn't keep driving the rental.

The truck wasn't new to anyone but him. It had a good engine, and even boasted leather seats, something Sam would probably bemoan come summer.

He found the red brick church on the corner of Buffalo Bill Road and Second Street, right where it had always been. Memories rushed at him. Darren pushing him as they walked behind their parents up the sidewalk. Church service to rip out all the bushes along the side of the building and replant flowers. Singing from the choir seats.

Peace flowed over Sam like warm rain, and he closed his eyes for a moment to send a prayer heavenward. He wasn't sure when he'd started petitioning God to bring Bonnie to Coral Canyon, but he found himself doing it again when he should've just expressed his gratitude and gotten himself inside the chapel.

He cut himself off mid-thought and whispered, "Help me," as an end to his prayer. The inside of the building smelled just as Sam remembered, like candle wax and antiseptic. The pastor was not the same, but Sam found his youthful face and bright eyes to be charming. The choir opened the meeting with *Christ the Lord is Risen Today*, and Sam's throat closed off. He made a wheezing sound as he pictured *his* choir in the stand.

His choir wore navy blue robes, not this strange magenta.

His choir sang so much better than this one.

His choir was performing this song last.

He glanced at his phone. His choir had already performed this song.

He couldn't sit here and listen to the wrong song being sung first. Thanking the Lord he'd chosen to sit in the back, Sam got right back up and left the chapel. He told himself as he drove away that he'd try to stay for ten minutes next week.

Misery followed him wherever he went. The swimming hole he'd frequented as a child was closed, the road flooded. With fury pounding through his veins, he turned back the way he'd come.

Bonnie did not send a video of the Easter program, though with the time difference, it should've ended hours ago. He'd never experienced such a level of helplessness.

"Sure you have," he muttered to himself, something he'd been doing a lot lately. He hadn't realized how quiet it was to live alone. How lonely a man got. How much he'd come to rely on having his brothers around to talk to when he wanted to.

"When Bonnie had her panic attack. You were helpless then." Sam was experiencing the same sensations now. His fingers tingled as if they'd been separated from his body. He literally had no idea what to do.

So he just drove. He drove north and west until he hit Yellowstone National Park. Then he turned around, bypassing Coral Canyon and kept going east as if he'd drive across the country right now and go straight to Bonnie's door.

He imagined himself showing up on her front porch, a dozen roses in his hand and a hopeful smile on his face. She'd open the door, and Boyfriend would sniff his knee just before Sam dropped onto it to propose.

Sam stalled the fantasy. He had no hope for him and Bonnie, and he wouldn't be driving to Island Park today. Or any day. At least not to see her.

He eased onto the shoulder and made a U-turn. Driving slowly, he didn't arrive back at the farmhouse for another hour. Misery came in with him and made itself comfortable right in the fleshy parts of his heart.

CHAPTER
NINETEEN

Bonnie endured the Easter program but she did not record it. Only five days had passed where she didn't hear Sam's voice, and every one was agony.

She made it through each hour of each day simply by reverting to muscle memory. She showered but couldn't remember if she'd used conditioner on her hair. Drove to work but didn't know if any of the stoplights she'd gone through had actually been green. Visited her mother but wasn't sure what they talked about by the time she got home.

She existed, the same way she had in the months following Jeff's death. She knew this type of living wasn't really living at all, but she couldn't make her own heart stop. She didn't even have all the pieces anymore. Some belonged to her ex-husband, somewhere off in Maine. Some belonged to Sam, many miles away. Some belonged to her son, buried in the cemetery. She tried going there to see if she could feel better, somehow make her whole chest stop aching, but it didn't work.

The after-school sun beat down on her and she ran her fingertips along the top of the headstone. Most of the snow had melted, and Bonnie prayed summer would bring her a better outlook on life. Only one more month of school. One more month of routine. Then what would she do to fill her days, drive Sam from her mind?

She turned away from her son's grave and lifted her eyes toward Steeple Ridge. Ten minutes later, she parked in their public lot, the one Sam said their customers used.

She had no idea where to go from there, but her feet took her into the barn. Music played from a room down the way, so she kept on going. She paused in the doorway of an office, where Missy Jenkins sat at a desk.

"Hey, Missy."

The other woman startled and stood. "Bonnie." She crossed to her quickly and drew her into a hug. Bonnie leaned into it, craving the touch of another human being so badly. Surely Michelle had hugged her over the past couple of weeks, but Bonnie couldn't remember.

"What are you doing here?" Missy asked.

"I want to take horseback riding lessons," Bonnie said, the words just suddenly there. "Not just in the arena like I sort of did over the winter. But outside." She took a big breath. "Outside under the sky."

Missy stepped back and looked at her with a curious expression. She finally said, "All right."

"Can I have Dandelion?"

"I'll have to check his schedule."

"And Darren." Bonnie wasn't asking this time. Though she thought it dangerous to work with a Buttars man, she craved the connection to Sam, even if it was stupid.

"Darren?"

"I know he gives horseback riding lessons. He's patient with me."

Missy returned to her desk and sat down. "Come fill out some forms. I'll go talk to Darren."

Half an hour later, Bonnie's stomach growled and she thought Missy had abandoned her. The music still warbled from the speakers in the ceiling, and the clomping of horse's hooves took her to the doorway.

Her heart stuttered, daring to hope she'd see Sam bringing in a horse from pasture. Of course she didn't. Tucker put the horse in his stall, stroked the steed's face, chuckled as he fed the animal something from his palm.

Bonnie walked toward him and lifted her hand to pat the horse too. "What's his name?"

"Oh, hey Bonnie. Missy said you were here." Tucker gave her a genuine smile. Not one of those filled with pity, sympathy, and a burning desire to know what had happened. He probably already knew what had happened, or a version of it anyway.

"I'm signing up for horseback riding lessons."

"Yeah. My wife and Darren are currently arguing about it in the back barn." Tucker flashed her another grin. "Missy'll win. She always does."

"Why are they arguing?"

"Oh, you know."

"No, I don't know. I'll pay for the lessons."

"I'd give them to you for free." Tucker twisted toward her and leaned into the stall door. "You know, if I could ride better than a ten-year-old." He chuckled but sobered just as quickly. "Darren's just...cautious. So serious and reserved. He doesn't want to get between you and Sam."

"There is no me and Sam," Bonnie said sharply. "And what would Darren giving me horseback riding lessons have to do with that?"

"Some of us think there is a you and Sam, and that you guys will find your way back to each other one day." Tucker shrugged and looped the reins he'd used to bring in the horse until they made a perfect circle. "Darren's one of them. I am too." He tipped his hat and turned to leave the barn.

Bonnie stood there, dumbfounded. When the surprise wore off, the frustration came. And when that had bubbled away, all that was left was anger. Her eyes landed on the placard bearing the name of the horse she still stroked. Journey.

Somehow, it spurred her into motion. She marched through the barn and outside. Just a few short strides and she'd reach the back barn, where she could hear voices. Male and female. Darren and Missy.

She entered the barn, where Missy said, "She *needs* this. You should know better than anyone how healing riding a horse can be."

Bonnie didn't hear Darren's response because of the adrenaline pounding through her ears. "Tucker said I could take Dandelion."

Darren swung toward her, and though Bonnie had seen the brothers briefly at church, the power of being this close to him hit her square in the chest. He was cut from a different cloth than Sam, but the sloped nose was the same. The strength in his shoulders. The pure confidence that oozed from him.

A sob wrenched her stomach, but Bonnie managed to keep it silent.

"Take him?" Missy said, coming around Darren to stand in front of him.

"Just out to the pasture," Bonnie said, wondering if the horse was even in the barn.

Missy exchanged one last look with Darren and approached Bonnie. "Come on. I'll let you see him." She looped her arm through Bonnie's and walked her outside, turned toward the pasture, and inhaled deliberately before saying, "Those Buttars brothers sure are stubborn."

Bonnie didn't know how to respond, so she simply kept putting one foot in front of the other. After a few minutes, Missy leaned up against a white, metal fence and whistled. The long, shrill sound seemed to go on forever, but when she finished, at least a half a dozen horses were coming their way.

Some trotted. Others plodded. Eventually the one with hair the color of freshly creamed butter arrived, and everything inside Bonnie unknotted as she touched the horse she'd come to love. "Hey, Dandelion. Did you miss me?"

I miss you.

Sam's text from weeks ago swam behind her eyes, which now burned with tears.

"Take as long as you want," Missy said before leaving Bonnie alone at Steeple Ridge Farm.

When she returned to her car, someone waited against the driver's door. Dusk had already fallen, and Bonnie's first reaction was to retreat to the farmhouse. But she strengthened her shoulders and wiped her eyes. So she'd cried out here. Big deal. People probably did it all the time. Sam had told her once about how he believed horses could heal unseen wounds, and she'd experienced it firsthand.

Maybe if she told Darren that, he'd give her the lessons. She approached slowly, her sandaled feet making hardly any noise on the dirt. "Evening, Darren," she said, employing her kindest voice. The closer she got, the more clearly she could see his face. He didn't look happy to see her, to be waiting for her. She wondered how long he'd been stalking her car.

"Look," he said, his voice not unkind but full of danger nonetheless. "I just—I mean—what am I supposed to tell Sam?"

Whatever Bonnie was expecting him to say, that wasn't it. "I don't care what you tell Sam." She reached into her purse and fished out her keys. Lifting her chin, she looked right into Darren's eyes. "I'm…lost. Okay? I'm lost. And I don't know if I'll find myself out here or not, but it's the one place I feel…less lost. And I love that stupid horse for some reason, and I just want to—"

"I'll do the lessons then," Darren said.

Bonnie blinked at him. "Okay," fell dumbly from her lips.

"But you have to bring Boyfriend out with you when

you come." He stomped a few feet away, finally opening a path for Bonnie to reach her car. "Logan's been moodier than Sam over the loss of that dog."

"Sam's been moody because of Boyfriend?"

Darren barked a laugh into the darkening sky and turned back to her. "Sam's been moody, depressed, indecisive, worried, you name it, over the loss of you."

"Maybe he should come home then."

Darren studied her for a few moments, but because of the distance and the darkness, she couldn't read his eyes. He finally said, "Maybe you should find yourself and then find him," and walked away.

———

BONNIE SCHEDULED HERSELF SOMETHING TO DO EVERYDAY after work that she hoped would transfer to her summer schedule too. She continued to see Dr. Huff on Mondays. Not only did Bonnie enjoy being able to truly express how she felt, she was beginning to make friends with the woman.

They'd spent a couple of weeks with Bonnie sobbing over Sam while Dr. Huff handed her tissues. Only a few words were said, but Dr. Huff's questions always took Bonnie several days—and sometimes longer—to untangle.

This week's had been, "What do you want your life to be?"

Bonnie's first instinct had been to say, "Happy." So she had. And Dr. Huff then asked her what she needed to be happy. Bonnie knew happiness was more than a feeling.

More than a fleeting moment. And she had no idea how to achieve it long-term.

Tuesdays, she visited her mother. And not just out of obligation or because she wanted to talk. But Bonnie started focusing on her mother, really paying attention to how she was feeling. On the last Tuesday before school got out, her mom asked, "What are you doing this summer?"

"Not much." Bonnie looked up from where she peeled potatoes into her mother's sink. "What about you?"

"I'm going to Florida."

Bonnie dropped the peeler into the sink, where it made a deafening clattering sound. "You are?"

"Jillian asked me to come a few weeks ago. I'm leaving next week."

Leaving next week. The words seemed to take forever to register in Bonnie's head. If Sam's house hadn't flooded, he would be leaving next week too. The past several weeks without him would've been completely different. Maybe Bonnie would be leaving Island Park too.

"Good for you, Mom." A sense of warmth and rightness covered Bonnie's skin. "When are you coming back? I can take care of the house while you're gone."

Mom stepped next to her at the sink and put her hand on Bonnie's peeling fingers. "I'm thinking about making the move permanent." She looked right into Bonnie's eyes, and Bonnie saw a sparkle there she hadn't in a while.

"Really?"

"It's awfully cold in Vermont in the winter. Florida might be a welcome change for my old bones." Mom smiled, a measure of sadness softening her gaze. "Plus, it's not healthy for me to stay here, cooped up in this old house I used to share with Daddy. I think I'm ready to let go." The pressure on Bonnie's hand increased as her mom squeezed. "Maybe you could do the same."

"What? Leave town? Go to Wyoming?"

"Yes, exactly."

Bonnie pressed her lips together and slipped her hand out from under her mother's. "I'm thinking about it."

"Seems like you've been doing that for a while now."

"It's complicated."

"I know it is, sweetie." Mom moved away, and Bonnie felt her slipping away more than just physically. "I know it is."

The next day, Bonnie went to the veterinary clinic after school to volunteer. Logan had given her the idea when he'd come to the school with two leashed dogs a few weeks ago. When she'd asked him what he was doing, he said he did pet therapy with the special needs students. Bonnie had no idea how she didn't know that had been happening "for months" as Logan claimed.

Bonnie had to really pause and examine her memories to find many from the past year. At the same time, some moments were so bright and vivid, Bonnie couldn't seem to think of much else. Like kissing Sam for the first time. Like sitting next to Sam at her father's funeral. Like holding Sam's hand while he slept on the airplane.

Those memories seemed branded in silver in her mind, while others she'd forgotten completely or shimmered softly around the edges.

Logan had said, "Layla can always use extra help on

Wednesdays," and Bonnie had shown up at the clinic the very next day. Layla had put her to work feeding the sheltered animals and organizing supplies. Work that was easy but kept Bonnie busy. After a month there, Bonnie had graduated to dog-walker, and she stopped by her house to get Boyfriend before she went to the clinic.

She and Layla had become fast friends too, and Bonnie's spirits lifted when she pushed through the back door of the clinic and found the bubbly brunette crouched in front of the largest Newfoundland dog Bonnie had ever seen.

"Hey, there." Layla stood and sent a huge smile in Bonnie's direction. "This is Mac. Got him in today from Burlington. He's just the sweetest. Aren't you? Aren't you the sweetest?" She scrubbed the dog, who seemed to smile up at her with pure bliss in his half-closed eyes. "He wants to walk with Boyfriend today."

Layla handed Bonnie the leash, and with two huge dogs that could surely pull her from here to the moon, she set out. She went down Center toward Main and headed for the park behind the courthouse. Boyfriend liked to chase the birds there, and most of the moms took their kids to other parks around town with more playground equipment.

She threw the dogs a ball and enjoyed watching them circle and chase each other, their tails wagging and the tongues lolling out of their mouths. When their time ended, she went around on the south side of the building and slowed when she saw a group standing on the corner, waiting to cross.

She'd been planning to go back up to Center and back to the veterinary clinic, but when she heard, "We have to get as much support at the hearing as possible," she changed her mind. She'd forgotten about the proposed fountain—surely that was what they were talking about. She wasn't sure if they were in favor of the fountain or not, but she gave them a placid smile and stepped with them when the light turned green.

They continued to chatter, but Bonnie couldn't get any information. So she said, "When is the hearing?"

"Two weeks," a man said. He looked like he wanted to say more but in the end, he turned and continued with his group. Bonnie went back to the clinic and watered the dogs. Layla's car was already gone, but the night janitorial staff was in the building, so Bonnie put Mac in his kennel and loaded Boyfriend in the backseat before heading home.

Bonnie played the piano on Thursdays. She'd re-enrolled herself in lessons, and she went to Valerie McDonnell's apartment near the hospital immediately following school. She'd seen a few students going in as she was leaving, but Bonnie had dismissed her feelings of inadequacy. She wanted to fill her time with good things, and playing the piano brought her joy.

And if she were being completely honest with herself, she felt closer to Sam when she played. Almost like he stood at her right shoulder in her den, the way he had a couple of times as they worked on the Easter program.

She missed Sam a lot on Thursdays, and she always stopped by La Ferrovia on her way home for spinach stuffed shells. She liked to think of him as she ate on her back patio, the chords and technique she'd refreshed that day still in her fingers, her heart, her soul.

But Friday was the day she longed for Sam. Ached to see him. Friday, she went out to Steeple Ridge for horseback riding lessons. She had to hear Darren speak in a voice very much like his brother's. See the farmhouse where she and Sam had shared a lot of meals, and some laughter, and maybe a kiss or two or three.

At the same time, Bonnie was slowly finding her way back to herself. With Dandelion's help, the aid of the fresh air, and the assistance of a big, beautiful sky, Bonnie could truly examine things while at Steeple Ridge.

She felt closer to God here than anywhere else, and she wondered if Sam had felt that spirit here too. Wondered if he had that same feeling on his farm in Coral Canyon. Wondered if she could.

She'd refrained from asking Darren about Sam. He'd made it clear he didn't want to be the gossip boy between them, that if she wanted to know how Sam was, or if he'd gotten the water out of his basement, she should talk directly to him. Bonnie wanted to, but her courage had wandered off about the time she'd broken down in church.

After parking in the public lot, she paused near the fence line and drew in a deep, deep drag of air. A rush of affection for this farm infected her bloodstream. *Thank you,* she sent toward heaven, grateful that even though she didn't have Sam currently in her life, she still had this farm. This farm she'd grown up only five miles from, had known about but had never visited, could see from her son's grave.

A nagging voice—*her* voice—inside her head reminded her that she'd first felt this spirit at Sam's farmhouse in Coral Canyon. She'd been praying for a solid month to know what to do about him. Her pleas had intensified over the past couple of days since discovering her standing Tuesday appointment to make dinner with her mother would only happen one more time.

Her mother, who'd lived in Island Park for sixty-eight years was leaving. Leaving her husband here. Leaving the house she loved. Leaving.

Why can't I leave too? Bonnie asked as she headed down the gravel path between the barn and the fenced pastures. She could ready Dandelion by herself now. In fact, Darren required it. She usually met him on the north end of the property and he'd give her instructions, demonstrate, help her into the saddle, and then call more corrections to her as she rode. Sometimes they worked in the indoor arena because of the evening heat, but she was moving her lesson time to the mornings starting next week.

"Dandelion," she cooed at the horse once she arrived at his stall. He came quickly to her and nudged her palm in hello. She giggled softly and pressed her forehead to the horse's. Such a gentle being, this horse.

Bonnie had never dared step into the main barn and visit Lady. She wasn't even sure if the white horse was still here, but she suspected it was. Sam would come for her himself, and Bonnie desperately wanted to know when so she could get on a train, a plane, anything to keep herself from coming out to Steeple Ridge to see him.

She saddled Dandelion and took him out to the pasture, where Darren waited for her. He looked tired, and hot, and growly, the way he always did. "Hey," she said, the reins held loosely in her hand the way he'd taught her.

"Evenin'." He managed a faint smile.

"Good week?"

"Good enough. You?"

"Last day of school today. So yeah, great week." She grinned at him and dropped the reins so she could gather her hair into a ponytail. "What are we doing today?"

"Just riding." He swung onto Paintbrush and looked at her.

"No lesson?"

"I think you're ready."

She turned toward Dandelion, who she hadn't quite mounted by herself. He seemed ten feet taller than he had mere seconds ago. She pushed off, swung her leg, and landed in the saddle. Laughter bubbled from her core, up her throat, and out of her mouth. "I did it."

Darren chuckled. "Bonnie, you can do anything, I think."

Bonnie wasn't so sure of that, but she accepted the cowgirl hat Darren had presented her with on the first lesson. His first lesson had been, "Never ride a horse without a hat," and Bonnie hadn't. The times with Sam didn't count, she'd decided, as she'd really just led Dandelion around the indoor arena and patted his cheeks.

Darren led her into the forest northwest of the farm,

skirting the cemetery. They didn't speak, something Bonnie appreciated. With the world seemingly gone, she let her mind wander. She tried to look at everything, take in the beauty of the browns, greens, blues, blacks, and a faint bit of red showing through the foliage.

She wasn't sure how much time passed, but when she looked for Darren again, she couldn't find him. "Darren?" She twisted in the saddle, but he wasn't behind her either.

A shout to her left caught her attention and she nearly fell off the horse's back as she turned that way. She gripped the reins tighter. "Come on, Dandelion," she said, employing as much bravery as she could.

"I'm coming!" she yelled. "Where are you?" She couldn't remember what Darren had been wearing— besides the white cowboy hat, of course. She'd never seen him without that.

"Bonnie!" he yelled, and she managed to point her horse in the right direction. She found him halfway down an embankment that looked like it had just been formed, struggling to get Paintbrush up.

Every step they took sent them further into the soft earth, and panic paraded across Darren's face. Bonnie's breath heaved in her chest. "Darren," she said. "What do I do?"

"You have a rope on your saddle," he said, panting. "Throw it to me. Then call Ben. Then call nine-one-one."

Bonnie's fingers fumbled over the rope. She had no idea how to throw it to him. She hadn't thrown anything in ages. He was a moving target, sliding sliding sliding.

"Come on, Bonnie," he said, his voice calm now.

"I can't—what if I miss?"

"I have faith you can do this."

He had faith.

Sam had faith.

Bonnie gripped the rope too tight, too tight. "Please guide the rope to Darren," she whispered right before she threw it.

The rope sailed through the air, and all sound ceased. He caught it, wrapped the end of it around the saddle horn, and threw it right back toward her. "Get it," he said. "Wrap it around a tree. Make the phone calls."

She slid from Dandelion's back. The horse pranced backward a few steps, sensing the danger at his hooftips. Bonnie scrambled for the rope, her feet getting stuck in the dirt and mud and dead, wet, moldy leaves left by the winter snows. She hurried around the closest tree and knotted the rope. She yanked her phone from her pocket and dialed Ben. After a breathless thirty-second conversation, she called dispatch. They wouldn't let her off the line, and as Bonnie stood at the top of a hill that was getting slipperier by the moment, her frustration grew.

She wanted to call Sam.

Sam should know his brother was in danger.

Sam would come and fix everything.

Standing there, waiting, watching as Ben and Logan and Tucker and Missy arrived and started throwing more ropes, Bonnie knew what she needed to do if she wanted to fix everything in her life.

Now she just needed the faith to do it.

CHAPTER
TWENTY

Sam listened to Ben talk and talk. When he finally stopped, Sam asked, "So Darren's all right?"

"He's a bit shaken," Ben said. "But don't tell him I told you that. He's got his tough-guy mask on."

"I do not!" Sam heard Darren yell, and he chuckled.

"Horses okay?" Sam asked.

"Everyone's fine," Ben said.

"Wow." Sam took off his cowboy hat and tossed it on the dining room table he'd only used as a storage shelf. "Sounds like an exciting day." He went into the bedroom and sank onto his bed to remove his boots. "How did Darren get a hold of you? We never have good service that far out. And why would he go out there alone?"

"He wasn't alone," Ben said, and though Sam wasn't in the same room as him, Sam heard a note in Ben's voice that set his alarms off.

"Who was he with?"

"A…woman."

"A woman?" Sam's interest in the conversation skyrocketed and he abandoned his boots. "Who was it?"

Ben sighed. "I don't want to tell you."

"Ben," Sam warned. "You tell me right now who Darren had out in the forest with him. Was it Sarah?"

"Sarah?" Ben's voice pitched too high, and Sam wished he was there at the farmhouse, especially because he knew Darren was closeby. Probably shaking his head and shooting a murderous glare at Ben.

A scuffle came through the line, and Sam caught Ben saying, "He should know, Darren," in a low voice.

"Darren?" Sam asked. "What's goin' on?"

"It was Bonnie Sherman," Darren said, his voice on bark mode. "She was with me. She threw me the rope. Called Ben. Called the police."

"Bonnie?" Sam almost added, "My Bonnie?" but there was nothing about her that was his. His heart twisted at the mere thought that she wasn't his, and his throat narrowed. Jealousy like he'd never known poured through him.

"She's been takin' horseback riding lessons for about six weeks," Darren said. "She was calm, and cool, and she saved the day."

"Horseback riding lessons?"

"Yeah. She comes every Friday." A loud clunk came through the line and Darren took a minute to come back on the line. "Ben is flapping his arms around. Made me drop the phone. *Fine*, Ben."

Sam waited for Darren to continue explaining. "Sometimes she comes out after church too. None of us mind. She says she…can find herself here."

Sam had no idea what that meant. Sounded like Darren didn't either. "So she's out there all the time?"

"I wouldn't say all the time."

"Are you dating her?"

"What?" Darren let two heartbeats go by. "Sam, I can't believe you think I would do that." He spoke in a freaky calm voice that set Sam's hair to standing.

"Of course not." Sam shook his head. He was out of his mind, that was all. He missed Bonnie, and every cell in his body wanted to see her ride a horse through the forest. Be with her when she did it. Pull her down, press her against a tree trunk, and kiss her.

He missed her so much. A long sigh came out, and he said, "I'm glad you're okay."

"You're still coming next weekend, right?"

"She comes out on Fridays?"

"Yes, but now that school's out, her lessons will be in the morning."

Sam was coming to get Lady, and he'd been planning to stay for a week, get everything else he needed, and drive back to Coral Canyon alone. Always alone.

"Yeah, I'm still coming." He didn't know when else he could. Once summer arrived at the farm, he had too much work to leave for a week.

"And to the wedding, right?" Ben asked, obviously not holding the phone.

"Yes, September fifth. I've got it on the calendar."

"Rae managed to convince the pastor to marry us at the sports complex."

"That's great."

"Yeah, great," Darren deadpanned. "How's the basement?"

"Still water-free, thank goodness." But really, Sam had been thanking the Lord for the past month of dryness in his basement. "The mold specialist is coming one more time on Monday. If it's clear again, I can patch the walls and get everything repainted."

"That's great," Darren said.

Sam's stomach growled, and he'd lost all his drive to make himself something for dinner. "I have to go. It's good to talk to you guys." His brothers said their good-byes and Sam hung up. Despite his need for food, he stayed seated on the bed for a few extra seconds.

Bonnie out at Steeple Ridge. Throwing ropes. Saving lives.

He shook his head as the fond feelings started to crowd into his chest. She'd never responded to his only text after the phone call that had changed everything. He didn't want to see her when he went home next week. All the wounds he'd carefully stapled together would blow wide open, and he couldn't afford the emotional damage that would do.

For two weeks, he'd typed texts to her he wouldn't send.

A month of lying in bed at night and wondering if she was still awake, thinking about him.

He'd managed to train himself not to check to see if

she'd texted. Even went so far as to delete her thread on his phone. He'd taught himself to think of other things in the soft moments before he fell asleep. Then his dreams weren't haunted by the woman he couldn't have.

He would not undo all that hard work. He'd make sure he didn't arrive at Steeple Ridge until at least noon. Then there'd be no way to accidentally run into her.

He went into the kitchen and pulled down the half-sheet of paper he'd picked up at the grocery store. It listed all the restaurants that delivered, and he ordered two sub sandwiches and a bag of chips.

He glanced around the farmhouse and went out onto the deck. He loved this land. Life here alone hadn't been easy, but it had gotten a twitch better with every passing day. And as soon as he could get a couple of farmhands to help, the overwhelming nature of the land would lessen.

As the sun arced behind the mountains, he allowed himself five minutes to entertain thoughts about Bonnie. He could picture the exact shade of red she had in her hair. The perfect curve of her lips. The way she tasted when he kissed her that first time.

He could not conjure up the sound of her voice as easily as he once had. His ribs seemed to collapse, crushing his heart. *Help her be happy,* he prayed. *Help me to be happy too.*

He'd already begged God to bring Bonnie to Coral Canyon. And she'd never come. Sam felt like he was giving up, like maybe he didn't have enough faith to get the blessings he wanted, like he'd failed everyone—

Bonnie, his brothers, his parents—by leaving Steeple Ridge.

He sighed and turned away from the glorious sunset, the same prayer in the back of his throat that had been there for years. "Lord, I don't know what I'm doing. Please help me."

God had done exactly that for a lot of years. He'd helped Sam find jobs all four brothers could do. He'd kept them together. He'd guided Sam in ways he hadn't even realized until he'd come to Coral Canyon and had to face every day by himself.

"He'll do it again," Sam told himself as the doorbell pealed, indicating that his food had arrived. But as Sam answered the door and paid the delivery driver, he couldn't help feeling like God had abandoned him here in the desolate state of Wyoming.

Again.

———

Sam's plane touched down roughly, jostling him in his seat and making his fingers tighten on the armrests uncomfortably. He really hated flying. The rental truck and trailer back to Wyoming was costing a significant amount of money, but he'd take that over flying again anytime soon.

He wondered how Girlfriend had done with such a precarious landing. He'd brought his new Aussiedoodle with him, mostly because she was the sweetest dog on the planet and he wanted to prove to Logan that some dogs liked everyone.

He went through getting his bags, getting his dog, getting the truck, and getting himself out of the big city in an even bigger truck. The drive to Steeple Ridge seemed to take half a blink, and he checked the time. Almost eleven.

"You hungry, girl?" He glanced at Girlfriend, who seemed to smile back at him with a wagging tail that meant, *Yes, let's eat pizza!*

He swung by the pizzeria, knowing the line would take a good half an hour at this time of day. He didn't care. Out here, he had nothing but time.

He took his pie across the street to the park, where he could let his pup play and run and potty, and he could eat. Girlfriend made fast friends with a dog twice her size and seemed to enjoy the run—and the extra bites of crust Sam fed her whenever she came when he called.

Properly pepperonied, he and Girlfriend made the five-mile drive to Steeple Ridge and pulled into the driveway. He took an extra breath to appreciate the charm of the white farmhouse and the brilliance of the green lawn that Missy had obviously been tending to.

There was something special about this farm. Maybe all farms, because he felt the same level of peace and tranquility here as he did at Coral Canyon.

"Well, we're here. Remember I told you about Rambo? He's usually nice to other dogs." He got out of the truck and let Girlfriend jump down. She tore around the yard once before coming back to his side, her eager face looking to him for direction.

He chuckled as he scrubbed her head and started for the barn straightaway. His brothers would be out there anyway, and he wanted to see Lady and introduce her to his girlfriend.

He'd just passed the side entrance of the back barn when a burst of laughter met his ears. Mostly masculine, but a vein of a female voice floated into his ears.

He seized. He knew that laugh. It had gone quiet in his ears, but with the reintroduction of it into his physical life, everything about Bonnie's voice came roaring back.

Boot steps came toward him, and every muscle in his body screamed at him to *run! Hide!* He couldn't move.

Darren appeared, his face alive and happy. Ben and Rae followed, and Sam second-guessed himself. Maybe it had been Rae laughing. Surely Bonnie was long gone by now. He cursed himself for not checking the public parking lot for her car.

Rae and Ben cleared the barn, and everything moved in slow motion after that. Bonnie came through the door, her hair glistening in the sun with a reddish halo around her face.

Sam actually groaned at the beauty he found in her face. Pain poured through him, wave after wave of it.

When Bonnie's eyes landed on him, she froze too. Her mouth widened, and the joy drained from her face.

The sight of Sam had dampened her mood.

He'd never felt worse.

As fast as time had slowed, it roared forward again. Darren's face filled his vision. Darren's mouth moved. Darren practically shoved Sam toward the main barn.

Sam heard nothing, felt nothing. By the time he reached the barn doors and turned around, Ben and Rae had herded Bonnie somewhere else.

Sam faced the long hallway before him. His lungs finally released and he sucked in new air. The scent of straw and horseflesh came with it, and Sam bent over, trying to figure out what had just happened.

Girlfriend whined, and Sam wanted to join her.

CHAPTER
TWENTY-ONE

onnie stared at Ben. "What do you mean he wasn't supposed to be here until later? You knew he was coming?"

Ben shrugged one shoulder and looked to Rae for help. "He came to get Lady," Rae said in a soothing voice, her eyes kind and anxious. "He's staying for a week."

"A week?" Bonnie couldn't avoid him for *a week*. She had appointments and visits and volunteering—and lessons. "So I can't come to the farm this week. Is that it?"

"You can come any time you want," Ben said.

Bonnie scoffed, her blood on fire. Sam couldn't be here. Not yet. Bonnie had only had a week to put her plans in motion, and she wasn't ready to see him. Not yet.

She paced away from Ben and Rae, ran her hands through her hair, and tried to think. She returned to her friends and said, "I need more time."

"More time for twhat?" Rae asked.

"I just started dejunking my house. I was going to put it up for sale."

A light entered her friend's eyes. "And then move to Wyoming?"

"Well, I was also working up the courage to call Sam, but yeah, Wyoming is the end goal."

Ben's mouth didn't seem to shut. He blinked, first at Bonnie and then Rae. "So you still like Sam."

Bonnie's face heated.

"She doesn't like Sam." Rae playfully punched her fiancé on the bicep. "Can't you tell? Bonnie *loooves* Sam." She giggled and wrapped her arms around Bonnie. "Right?" she whispered. "You're totally in love with him."

Bonnie hadn't quite admitted to herself that she was in love with Sam. Mostly because she was worried that by the time she'd sold her house, packed everything she owned, and got up the gumption to call him, he'd have moved on. Found himself another girlfriend.

"I think so," Bonnie whispered back. She stepped away, her hands automatically going around themselves. "What do I do now?"

"You march over there and tell him," Rae said, looking at Ben. "Right, Ben?"

"Rae flew to Wyoming to tell me." He gazed at her with such adoration, it made Bonnie's heart happy. "So yeah, I think you can get over to the other barn and let him know."

"What if he's moved on?"

Ben laughed, the sound filling up the smaller barn and

collecting in the rafters. "You must not know Sam as well as I thought you did. He mulls over everything for*ever*."

Bonnie did know. But she was also ready to be strong. She'd spent the last week cleaning out her house, and the realtor was set to come on Monday. She'd mapped the route to Wyoming. She'd told her mother, who had wept with her. Sad weeping for the people they'd be leaving behind in Island Park. Happy weeping that Bonnie could have a future filled with happiness instead of the façade of happiness.

Michelle had brought boxes from school, and Cheryl was bringing smoothies on Tuesday morning and then helping her pack.

Bonnie honestly hadn't thought much about how or when she'd tell Sam. She was beginning to realize that the Lord had a hand in everything—including when a house flooded, and when an embankment slid down, and when she should make a phone call. Big things, little things, it didn't matter. The evidence of God existed everywhere, and Bonnie was trying to be more reliant on Him than she'd been in the past.

"Hat or no hat?" she asked Rae, putting on her cowgirl hat and then taking it off again.

"No hat," Rae said.

"I'm so nervous." Bonnie tossed the hat onto a wooden box near the door where she stood.

"Relax," Rae said. "It's *Sam*."

"Exactly," Bonnie muttered before turning and entering the June sunshine. Darren had pushed Sam into the main barn, where she now knew he'd been going to see Lady.

She'd also noticed an unfamiliar dog with him, and she wondered what that was all about, and why Boyfriend hadn't barked his head off at the new arrival yet.

She entered the barn and her eyes betrayed her, making everything black. They adjusted as she stepped. The closer she drew to Lady's stall, the louder the male voices got until she heard Sam say, "This is my girlfriend."

Bonnie gasped, blinked rapidly, and fell back a step. She hadn't noticed another woman with Sam, but she could've already been in the barn. Or she could've stopped by the farmhouse to use the restroom.

A puppy barked, a high-pitched noise that aggravated Bonnie.

"Hush," Sam said. "This is Lady. You two are gonna have to figure out how to get along."

"I can't believe you named your dog Girlfriend." Darren chuckled. "Logan is gonna be so mad."

"Why?" Sam asked. "Just because his dog is a menace."

Relief raced through Bonnie's veins. At the same time, she did not appreciate the tricky terminology—not when it was being used on her. She proceeded toward Sam and Darren, making her footsteps heavier now so they'd hear her.

Darren turned her way, clapped his hand on his brother's shoulder, and high-tailed it out of the barn. *So much for easing into a conversation,* Bonnie thought.

She continued anyway, the mere sight of Sam so wonderful she thought she might faint. "So you brought your girlfriend?"

"I've only had her a month," Sam said, his gaze focused on the horse. "I couldn't leave her."

Bonnie winced. Sam seemed to realize what he'd said at the same time. "I mean— "

"It's fine, Sam," she said. "I know what you meant." She folded her arms as if the barn radiated a chill. The oxygen she inhaled felt like bleach in her lungs. "Sam, I put my house up for sale."

That got him to look away from the blasted horse. His hands stilled and everything. He studied her and oh, she loved the depth of his eyes. She loved the handsome lines of his face. Loved that his throat worked, but he didn't say anything because he was probably overthinking it.

The way she was.

"I'm in love with you," she said. Just like that. Opened her mouth and the words came out. "I don't belong here without you, so I decided to sell my house and move to this little farming town in Wyoming."

Sam didn't hesitate, and he apparently didn't need to think about what to do next, because he swept Bonnie into his arms, whispered, "I'm in love with you too," and kissed her.

CHAPTER
TWENTY-TWO

Sam kissed Bonnie with all the feeling he could muster. How he'd ever thought he could survive without her was insane. He hadn't been living these past few months. He'd simply been breathing, walking, eating.

But kissing Bonnie…. Kissing Bonnie was what living felt like. He cradled her face in his hands and pulled away. "I'm…I don't even know what I am." He matched his lips to hers again, and she melted into his touch, sending love and warmth down to Sam's toes and up to the top of his head.

She loved him.

He chuckled and broke their connection. "I was just comin' to get my horse."

She tucked herself against his chest, her arms strong and tight around his back. "Yeah, well, I need help getting my house ready to list, and you're just the man to do it."

"I am, huh?"

"You don't have a job, and you're big and strong." She stepped away from him, a blazing smile on her face that lit up everything inside of Sam. "Yep, I think you're the man for the job."

He couldn't help the soft smile that sat on his face. "I love you."

She threaded her fingers through his and said, "I love you, too." She ducked her head and tugged him away from Lady's stall. "Let's walk."

Sam went, because he wanted to be where Bonnie was. Wanted to keep touching her. Wanted to work out everything between them. He hadn't been isolated so long that when a woman said, "Let's walk," she really meant, "Let's talk."

"C'mon, Girlfriend," he said to his dog, and she trotted alongside him. "Where's Boyfriend?"

"Probably lounging on the couch with Rambo. Logan spoils them both."

Sam agreed, and he let Bonnie take the lead. She bypassed the farmhouse and his rental truck, setting them on a course for the cemetery to the north. Several minutes passed with only the whispers of the wind and Girlfriend's clickety-claws on the pavement between them.

"I'm sorry I didn't record the Easter program," she said.

Sam's throat tightened and released. "It's okay."

"No, I said I would, and I didn't, and that's not okay."

"Sometimes things happen." Sam focused on the horizon, flashes of things that had happened zipping through his mind. His parents' plane crash. The house flooding. Her son's death. Truth was, sometimes things did just happen. Things no one could control.

"You know I meant to come back, right?" he asked. "I couldn't help what happened at the house in Wyoming."

"I know." But her voice was almost stolen by the breeze.

Sam didn't know what else to do to fix what he'd done. So he simply said, "I'm sorry, Bonnie."

"It's not your fault," she said. "Like you said, sometimes things just happen." She inhaled and exhaled. "It was actually good for me. I needed some time to figure things out on my own." She glanced toward town, where the faint outline of buildings could be seen. "I am going to miss this place. My friends. I even like my therapist."

"You still doin' that?"

"Every week." She met his gaze with a hint of worry in hers. "It really helps."

Sam squeezed her hand. "I'm glad." The breeze kicked up and tried to steal his cowboy hat. He mashed it back on his head and looked around for his dog. He found her several paces back, sniffing something on the side of the road. He grinned at her.

"I'm glad you found a dog you like," Bonnie said.

"Do you think she and Boyfriend will get along?"

"Yeah, sure." Bonnie waved her free hand. "Boyfriend likes everyone, and everyone likes Boyfriend."

Such contentment spread through Sam, but he knew they had some rough conversations to get through. "Hey, what about your mom?" Sam asked. "You didn't say you were going to miss her. Is she coming to Wyoming with you?"

"She's moving to Florida." Bonnie's voice held notes of sadness, and Sam almost stopped walking.

"Florida?"

"My cousin lives there. She invited her to come, and Mom's always hated the winters here." She paused, her throat working as she swallowed. "She left on Tuesday. I'm getting her house ready to sell too."

"Wow, that's a lot of change." He wondered if Bonnie was really doing as well as she seemed. She'd changed a little in the three months he'd been gone. Changed, but she still wonderful. She seemed stronger, more sure of herself and what she wanted.

"It's going to take me a few months."

"So I'll be going back to Coral Canyon alone next week." Sam's heart deflated the tiniest bit, though it was ridiculous to assume she could box up her entire life in less than a week.

"Probably." She tucked her hand into his elbow and leaned into him. "But we can talk, the way we did when you first went. I'll get everything sewn up here and join you out there."

Sam rarely let his uncensored thoughts out of his mouth, but "And then what?" just flew from his lips.

"Then we, you know…."

"No, I don't know. Are you going to get a job? Where will you live?" He stopped walking and looked at her. Really looked. Tried to see right inside her soul. "I want to get married." His words scratched his throat the tiniest bit. "Do you want to marry me, Bonnie?"

"Are you asking me right now?"

"No," he said, thinking of all the ways he'd imagined his proposal would go. Standing out in the middle of a deserted street hadn't been present in those dreams. No ring. No, he wasn't asking her right now.

"I'm just asking you if you think you'd like to marry me."

Her eyes sparkled. "Oh, you don't want to have to wonder what I'll say when you do propose, is that it?"

"Yeah, that's it," Sam said in a completely sarcastic voice. He started walking again.

"I'd like to marry you," she said, and a grin popped onto Sam's face. He paused again, this time to lift her off her feet and kiss her.

She giggled, and held onto his shoulders, and everything in Sam's world was exactly how it should be.

———

By the time Sam loaded Lady into the horse trailer a week later, every muscle in his body was looking forward to a very long drive, where he could just sit. No lifting boxes. No carrying furniture down stairs and out narrow doorways. No more scrubbing blinds, and patching walls, and climbing onto roofs.

Bonnie sure knew how to work, and she had her house cleaned out, with most of her stuff in storage, and ready to list by Wednesday. Then they'd immediately started on her mother's house—which was a much different beast. Thankfully, the woman had already left for Florida, because Sam thought she might have some hoarding tendencies, what with the porcelain dolls and silver spoons and stamps. He'd never seen so many stamps!

Bonnie had told him it was her father's stamp collection, and she'd handled it with reverence and care, placing it in a water-proof box and personally driving it over to the storage unit.

He'd only been able to help for two days on her mom's house before he had to get back to Coral Canyon. He had his lady in the trailer, all of his clothes and other personal items boxed and in the back of the truck, and his girlfriend waiting for him on the bench seat.

All he had left to do was say good-bye to Bonnie. He didn't know how to say the words. He didn't know when he'd be back, or how quickly her house would sell. They'd talked a lot about marriage and when—and where—they might do that, but no definite plans had been made.

She waited for him at the edge of the pasture, where her beloved Dandelion grazed.

"Hey." He joined her, resting his elbows on the top rung of the fence.

"Got everything loaded up?" She trained her beautiful eyes on him, and he lost himself to her again. He wondered if he'd always feel this much love for her when he looked at her. He hoped so.

"Yep. Lady went right in like a champ."

Bonnie laid her head on Sam's shoulder and sighed. "So I'll call you tonight."

Sam nodded, his voice box infected with emotion. When it finally loosened, he said, "I want to know everything that's happening with the houses."

"Mine went on the market this morning. There's an open house tomorrow. Edgar is hopeful we'll get a lot of people through and we can sell it quickly."

Sam didn't know the real estate agent the way Bonnie did. But all he could do was trust him. Trust in the Lord. "And then you'll come."

"About that."

Sam jerked like he'd been electrocuted. "What do you mean, 'about that'? You're coming to Coral Canyon when your house sells. Right?" He stared at her, trying to see her thoughts inside her head.

"I think we should get married first."

"Before you come?"

"Yes. It doesn't make sense for me to find somewhere to live when you've got that big old farmhouse all to yourself." She cocked her head and studied him, concern swimming in her gaze. "Does that make sense to you?"

It certainly didn't. Sam had spent countless hours standing on the back deck, staring at the Teton Mountains, imagining Bonnie living in the farmhouse with him. He wanted her there. Wished she were coming with him today.

"Maybe Ben would let us get married with him and Rae," Sam said.

"That won't work," Bonnie said. "They're getting married at the sports complex."

"And it's not for three more months."

"I've been married before," Bonnie said. "I've had a big wedding. I'll do whatever you want. I just need a few days to get my mother here and find a dress."

Sam's mind churned and churned. "I wish I'd known that a few days ago."

Bonnie giggled and clutched his arm a little tighter. "I can't go right now anyway. I have to sell two houses."

"Yeah, I know." Sam straightened, pushing out his breath as he did. "Well, I should hit the road, sweetheart. I have a long way to go to get to Toronto with a horse trailer."

She gazed up at him, and Sam could see the love in her eyes. Feel it in her touch as she swept her fingers across his jaw. "I think you should forget your razor more often," she said just before tipping up on her toes to kiss him.

Sam didn't think a good-bye kiss could be so sweet.

CHAPTER
TWENTY-THREE

Bonnie slicked her palms down the front of her shorts, wishing she were anywhere but in the city council room. She wasn't sure if she'd speak tonight, but she watched the workers get the microphones set up for the public hearing about the fountain on Main Street.

A dozen or so people had already arrived, but the room continued to fill as the minutes passed. Bonnie felt light-headed. Images flashed through her mind, but she worked to control them, the way Dr. Huff had been teaching her.

The panic subsided as quickly as it had come, and Bonnie wiped her forehead and took a deep breath. She wouldn't relive that day again. She couldn't blame herself forever. At least Dr. Huff said she couldn't.

Sometimes things just happen.

Bonnie calmed further with Sam's voice in her head. He'd told her to call as soon as the meeting ended, no matter what time. He'd said a lot of things over the past few days since he'd left.

Any news on the house?

Bonnie had no news. The house had only been on the market for four days, and her real estate agent had shown it to several people.

Are you lookin' for a wedding dress?

Bonnie hadn't been.

I think you should. Once that house sells, I'm gonna want you here.

Bonnie smiled as the meeting began. The sound of the mayor's voice erased Sam's, and she sat up straighter. They went through meaningless city business, and then got to the part everyone had crammed into the room to hear.

"We'll now hear public opinion on the proposed water feature located at one-fifty-two south Main Street."

Bonnie scoffed at "water feature". The last thing this town needed was more open water for a child to fall into. The lake that bordered the town was enough. People could go there to get their feet wet.

A line formed at the microphone, and Bonnie simply folded her arms. She wasn't sure if her opinion counted or not, and she kept telling herself she wouldn't be raising her next child in this town.

After hearing how it would beautify and add variety to the downtown area, as well as the wasteful nature of such an item, Bonnie decided to get up and speak. Her insides quaked as she waited in line, and it seemed like a hush fell on the crowd when it was finally her turn.

She hadn't planned anything, and she opened her mouth to speak. Nothing came out. She cleared her throat and tried again. "My name is Bonnie Sherman. I've lived in Island Park my whole life."

A strong, swift surge of emotion hit her. She wouldn't be living here much longer. Wouldn't be able to wander the streets and experience her childhood memories. She drew a breath and glanced down the row of city council members, as well as other city personnel, and finally the crowd.

"Some of you may know that my four-year-old son drowned in the pond at the Lakeside Sports Complex almost six years ago."

Of course everyone knew. The mayor had been mayor then too.

"I don't think anyone should ever have to go through what me and my family went through. I don't think our public money should be spent on an open water feature, without supervision, railings, or other preventative measures. Things happen. Sometimes those things are bad. It doesn't make a person bad, or imply that they did something wrong, or that they should've done something different." As she spoke, a heavy burden she'd been carrying for many long years lifted. She couldn't believe how light she felt, how easy it was to hold herself up and keep breathing. Those things had required so much effort for so long.

But the self-forgiveness was freeing. Fabulous.

"Sometimes things just happen," she repeated. "But there are things we *can* control to make the risks less severe. And I believe this city council has the ability to *not* approve this fountain, in the hopes that another child will not lose his life, and another family won't be broken. Thank you."

She returned to her seat, her heart thumping and jumping in her chest. Her vision blurred with unshed tears. Someone reached over and touched her hand. Another smiled at her. Bonnie let her tears fall, something she'd only allowed to happen behind closed doors with Dr. Huff.

But here, now, she didn't care. Because finally feeling like she could truly put Jeff to rest required tears. And that was okay.

———

"BONNIE, HOW DID THE MEETING GO?" SAM'S VOICE WAS LIKE a balm to her weary soul.

"Not approved," Bonnie said with a laugh as she turned onto the street and headed south. "And you wouldn't believe it, but I got up and spoke."

"You're right. I don't quite believe that."

"Right into the microphone and everything."

He chuckled and something banged on his end of the line. "Good job, sweetheart."

"How's the farm?"

"Exhausting," he said. "But in a good way. Got the posts in for the horse corral, and the hay's growing nicely."

"I also have some news on the house."

Sam sucked in a breath. "All right. Let me sit down first." He half-exhaled, half-groaned. "Okay, shoot."

"I got an offer."

He whooped. "That's great."

"I don't think I'm going to take it."

"What? Why not?"

"Guess who it's from?"

"Who?"

"Tucker and Missy." She pulled into her driveway and put the car in park.

"So?"

"So? *So?* They don't need this house. They have a house that's ten times nicer and bigger on the other side of town."

"Who cares? Sell it to them and get yourself out here so we can get married."

"No," Bonnie said, enjoying the playful banter between them.

"No?"

"*No,* you said you'd come here to get married."

"Fine, sell them the house, and I'll get myself back there so we can get married."

"I don't think so."

Sam emitted a long, drawn-out hiss.

"As far as I can tell, and I'm looking at my left hand at this very moment, I'm not even engaged."

"Ah."

Bonnie waited for more. Waited. Waited. Sam said nothing.

It was her turn to sigh excessively. "So you see, it feels premature to be planning a big wedding and a move across the country."

"Nice try. You already said you didn't want a big wedding."

"I would like a wedding ring." She'd taken the one Paul had bought for her and buried it deep in the ground near Jeff's headstone. She hadn't known what to do with it, and Paul said he didn't want it back. Bonnie figured everything had died the day Jeff had, so she'd put the diamond there the Sunday after Paul had left.

"I'm sure you would, Bonnie."

"People don't get married without rings, Sam."

"No, they don't." He laughed, the sound wonderful and welcome in her ears. "Sell the house, Bonnie."

"Okay." But worry seethed beneath Bonnie's skin as she got out of the car and walked up the sidewalk to her front door. "Why do you think they offered?"

"I don't much care, Bonnie. And you shouldn't either. Tucker has billions of dollars. Billions with a B. Sell him the house. Please."

Bonnie hated the level of desperation in Sam's voice. At the same time, she understood it. She didn't like being two thousand miles away from him either, not when she knew he loved her and wanted to be with her.

"Okay, Sam. I'll sell the house to Tucker." She twisted the doorknob and entered the house, where Boyfriend practically mobbed her.

The conversation moved on to dogs, and how Sam could keep Girlfriend from chasing the chickens. Bonnie hung up after several minutes of laughing at his stories of feathers and puppies, an intense well of missing in her core.

She fed Boyfriend while she hummed a tune she'd picked up somewhere, then she put together a plate of toast and fruit for herself. She should call Edgar back, tell him she'd love to accept Tucker's offer on the house.

Her phone sat on the counter, where she eyed it like it might transform into a snake and bite her. She ate methodically, in the silence, her brain battling with her heart.

In the end, she didn't call Edgar. She picked up her phone, reshouldered her purse, and pulled out her keys. Several minutes later, she sat in Tucker and Missy's driveway. Their house was definitely nicer than hers. Newer too. Nothing about her house would appeal to them.

Why had they offered on it then?

If Bonnie wanted to find out, she'd need to get herself out of the car and up to the front door. By God's grace, she did, and when Tucker answered the door, the surprise on his face was very easy to find.

"Bonnie." He stepped back and gestured for her to come in. "Missy, Bonnie's here."

"Already?" Missy poked her head up from where she worked on a black laptop at the dining room table. She bolted to her feet. "I mean– " She exchanged a glance with Tucker. "Bonnie, good to see you."

Bonnie thought Missy had enunciated her words a little bit too much, and she definitely had a vibe buzzing through her that something wasn't normal here. Maybe she shouldn't have come. Maybe buyers and sellers didn't do this. Some sort of real estate etiquette Bonnie didn't know.

"I just, oh, hey." She returned Missy's hug while Tucker

edged toward the kitchen. He pulled out a couple bottles of water and set them on the counter, then turned to get something else out of the cupboard.

Missy said, "I'm glad you came," in such a cheerful voice that Bonnie refocused on her. "Come sit down." Missy led her right past the most comfortable furniture in the house and into the dining room. "You sit here. No!" Missy waved both of her hands. "Over there."

"Missy," Tucker said in an exasperated tone.

"It's okay," she said. "I'm okay."

But Bonnie didn't think she was. She tried to get a read on Tucker, but he leaned against the kitchen counter and looked at his phone like he didn't have a care in the world. She took the chair Missy wanted her to—all the way around the table, in front of the window, and kitty-corner to where Missy repositioned herself in front of the laptop.

"So I came over," Bonnie said. "Because my realtor said you guys put an offer in on my house." She glanced at Tucker, a tall man who oozed confidence and charm, as he sat across from her. "I don't understand why. This house is much nicer than mine."

"Missy?" Tucker said.

"Two seconds," she muttered. "Just…another…click." She glanced up, beaming. "Got it."

Nothing the two of them were doing or saying made sense. Missy turned the computer toward Bonnie and pointed at it. "This is why we want to buy the house."

Bonnie looked at the screen—and saw Sam's handsome face. Her heart kicked to get free; a smile bloomed on her face; confusion needled her every brain cell. "Sam?"

"Hey, beautiful." He waved at her, his voice metallic through the laptop speakers. "I knew you'd come talk to Tucker and Missy about the house, and I believe just a half an hour ago you said you wanted a ring. So…."

Tucker slid something across the table toward Bonnie. She glanced at the black ring box, already open, and sucked in a breath. Fear mingled with excitement inside her. "Sam Buttars."

"Bonnie Sherman, will you marry me?" He grinned for all he was worth, and Bonnie picked up the box. The ring was rose gold—her favorite—and the diamond seemed to be the size of a golf ball. She ran her fingertip around it, hardly daring to contemplate how much her life had changed in only six months.

"It's lovely," she said.

"That's not a yes."

Bonnie laughed and tugged the ring free from its box. "I really like it." She gazed into the computer screen. "I really like you." She met Missy's eyes and then Tucker's. "But you can't buy my house just so I'll marry Sam."

"Of course we can," Tucker said, like he bought houses every day of the year. Maybe he did.

"You're miserable here without him," Missy said.

"Not true," Bonnie said, looking at Sam again. "I've been doing okay."

"You were doing okay when you thought you were broken up," Missy said. "But he's been gone four days, and you're a mess."

"I'm not," Bonnie said. "Sam, I'm fine."

"I'm not," he said. "I'm dying a slow death here

without you." He fake-coughed, which made Bonnie smile and a flood of warmth to heat her veins.

"You guys...."

Tucker leaned forward, his serious face in place. "Bonnie. Let me buy the house. Let Sam come home and marry you. Let yourself be happy."

Bonnie looked at the ring, so shiny and sparkly and shimmering. She looked at Missy, who said, "He paid off all my credit card debt. I get that you think you don't deserve it, or that you can solve your own problems, or whatever. But just let us do this for you."

Bonnie gazed at Sam. Her beautiful, bold, faithful, fantastic Sam.

"Okay," she said.

ONE MONTH LATER

Sam's awareness came back in slow intervals. He heard something click outside his dreams. He became aware of the air conditioner kicking on. He realized how light it was behind his eyelids. He shifted in bed, his hand brushing something foreign and soft.

He jerked back, fully awake now. His eyes flew open, and his heart catapulted to the back of his throat. Only a single second passed before he remembered he didn't sleep alone anymore.

A smile curved his mouth, and he edged closer to his wife, who hated early mornings as much as she hated sci-fi movies. He kissed her forehead anyway. She moaned, and he slid his lips to her ear.

"Stop it," she mumbled, still half-asleep.

Sam chuckled. "I like waking up next to you," he murmured before kissing her just below her earlobe. "It still kind of freaks me out, but I like it." When he finally moved his mouth to hers, he found her smiling and more than willing to let him kiss her good morning.

They'd only been married for a week, and only back in the farmhouse for two days. Sam had loads of work to do around the farm, as he'd been gone during the height of summer, when the most needed to be done.

So as much as he'd like to stay in bed and kiss his wife, he pulled himself from the warmth of her embrace and stepped into the shower. When he emerged from the bedroom, ready for a day of work, he found hot coffee in the pot and an empty house.

He fixed himself a cup of coffee and stepped onto the back deck. Bonnie stood in the yard while Boyfriend and Girlfriend ran after a ball. Girlfriend always got to it first, and Bonnie said, "Bring it back!" for the Aussiedoodle.

The pup sprinted back toward Bonnie while Boyfriend continued to sniff out something in the lawn. The sun had started to come up, but the roof of the farmhouse blocked it. Sam could see the golden light on the Grand Tetons before him, a beautiful, beautiful sight that soothed his soul whenever he looked west.

But the best sight of all was his beautiful, beautiful Bonnie walking up the stairs with the dogs at her heels. She came to stand beside him, and Girlfriend collapsed at his feet, and Sam thanked the Lord for such good blessings in his life.

———

Read on for a sneak peek at **HER MISTLETOE COWBOY**, the next book in the Steeple Ridge Romance series.

Order it in ebook, paperback, or audiobook by scanning the QR code below.

SNEAK PEEK! HER MISTLETOE COWBOY CHAPTER ONE

"Logan, Ben needs you."

Logan smiled at the woman who'd come to get him. He thought it was one of Rae's friends, someone from the rec center. She had hair halfway between blonde and red, and she practically wilted under Logan's smile.

He wiped it away as soon as he went past her. He wouldn't be getting a date while at his brother's wedding. Oh no. Today was all about Ben and Rae—and everyone else in Island Park, as it seemed the whole blasted town had shown up for the nuptials.

"Ben?" He pushed into the shed in the corner of the huge Sports Complex where Rae had insisted they get married.

"Over here. I can't tie this stupid thing." Ben sounded frustrated and nervous at the same time. Logan didn't blame him. When their oldest brother's plane had been delayed by two hours because of a freak hailstorm in Wyoming, both Ben and Logan had grown concerned.

Logan crossed the concrete to Ben. "He's going to get here." Sam was supposed to be the one helping Ben get dressed. Making sure every button was done up right, and the bow tie got proper square tips.

"Have you heard from him?"

"Yeah, they touched down an hour ago."

"The wedding is in thirty minutes."

"Well, probably sixty." Logan grinned at Ben, who stared at him with a hint of danger in his eyes. "Relax, Ben. Everyone's fine. You should see them sucking down that punch Rae won't give us the recipe for."

That got Ben to smile. "It's just almond flavoring."

"If that were true." Logan focused on the bow tie and got it looking decent. "She'd tell us the recipe."

"I'll get it out of her eventually."

Logan chuckled. "Right. Because married couples don't have secrets."

"I swear, we don't," Ben said. "It's just the punch, which she claims isn't really her recipe to give out. It's her mother's."

"And you're not married yet," Logan said. "So it's okay if Rae has secrets still."

"She doesn't have secrets," Ben insisted, which only made Logan smile wider. He loved teasing his brothers, especially Ben.

Logan stepped back and scanned his brother. "Looks good, bro. Nice and pressed."

Ben tugged at the sleeves of his jacket. "It's hot."

"You're the one who chose the first weekend of September to get married."

"That was Rae. She said the park would be amazing in the fall."

Logan shook his head and clucked his tongue. "Blaming her already."

Ben gave Logan a playful shove. "Go on. Get out of here. Go make sure we don't run out of punch." He tacked on a laugh, and Logan went because Darren came in. "He's nervous," Logan whispered to his twin as he passed.

Darren simply nodded. The more serious of the two, Darren had stepped up to take care of everything since Sam had gotten married and left town a couple of months ago. An intense wave of missing hit Logan right in the chest, where he struggled to breathe against it. But breathe he did, because he spotted Rae's mother and he was determined to get that punch recipe before the ceremony began.

"This is the best punch I've ever tasted," he said in a booming voice that echoed under the tents that had been set up. "Rae tells me it's your recipe."

Beth Cantwell smiled at him. "It sure is."

"So we're almost family now." Logan downed a mouthful of punch, the craving to do so again immediate and intense. There was definitely more in this punch than simply almond flavoring. The carbonation pinged against his throat as he swallowed.

"That we are." Beth continued talking, but her words fell into Logan's deaf ears. He blinked, and where there had once been a sea of people, now there only existed Layla Guyman.

She wore a floor-length gown the color of midnight, and Logan's mouth turned as dry as the Sahara. This wasn't the first time he'd had this reaction to the curvy blonde veterinarian. Oh no. He'd nearly rammed into the doorway at the church the first time he'd seen her. The second had almost left him with a broken toe as he'd lifted his foot to step onto the curb and didn't quite get his leg high enough.

She'd seemed interested in him too, but she'd pulled back, back, back, until Logan figured she wasn't. He'd put his feelings in a box on a shelf in the back of his mind, but they'd burst free at the sight of her so-blonde-it-was-almost-white hair swept off her neck and into a wedding up-do to out-do all other up-do's. Her skin had been kissed by the summer sun, and Logan wanted to touch her arm, hold her hand, skate his fingers along her jaw before he kissed her. Even from across the distance, he found the joy and sparkle in her intense blue eyes, and he suddenly wanted her gaze on his.

"Who are you starin' at?"

Logan clamped his mouth shut and startled, nearly spilling his almond concoction down the front of his suit. "No one." He glanced at Tucker, who'd appeared out of nowhere. Tucker, who now scanned the crowd where Logan had indeed been staring.

"Where's Missy?" Logan asked, hoping to distract his boss.

"You know, you should've excused yourself before drifting off into a stare-fest," Tucker said, completely undeterred.

"What are you talking about?"

"You were talking to Rae's mother. Now she thinks you might have special needs, because you just, and I quote, 'sort of went mute' and she 'couldn't get your attention'." Tucker sipped from his own glass of punch. "So who was it? Rita?"

Logan pressed his lips together. Rita had brown hair. Not bad brown hair, but Logan much preferred blondes.

"Not Rita. Okay." Tucker took longer to look at the crowd mingling under the tents. Logan had never wanted Sam to show up as badly as he did right now. But Sam was probably still at least forty-five minutes away, and there weren't all that many women for Tucker to choose from.

Thankfully, Tucker had only named four women before his wife joined them. "Tucker, have you heard from Sam?"

"No." He looked at Logan. "You?"

"He texted when they landed. He should be here in about thirty minutes." Logan started to edge away from Tucker and Missy, but the glint in Tucker's eyes meant he hadn't forgotten about Logan's "special needs" behavior.

He found Rae's mother and said, "I'm so sorry, Miss Beth. I saw someone I hadn't in a while, and I sort of zoned out."

She accepted his apology with grace but made a hasty escape with a silver-haired man Logan had never seen before. He sighed as he turned, planning to get more punch and find the coolest patch of shade he could.

He ran right into Layla instead. "Oof," he grunted at the same time she exclaimed, "Oh!"

He reached out and put his hand on her shoulder to

steady her, one of his fantasies roaring to life. Her skin against his fingers felt like silk and magic, and Logan lost his voice completely.

This is Layla, he told himself. They'd been friends for two years, even though she'd gone through a cold spell with him. He volunteered at the veterinary clinic where Layla worked twice a week. He saw her all the time at church functions, at work, around town.

But he'd never seen her like this.

"Nothing spilled." She scanned herself and then lifted her eyes to his, her glorious smile lighting up the entire park. "So we're good."

"Good," Logan echoed stupidly, wondering why his feelings for Layla had to be so present today of all days. He cleared his throat and tried to center his thoughts. He'd dated before. Women didn't scare him.

Layla sure did though. He managed to ask, "Have you tried that almond punch?"

"I've had it loads of times," she said. "I still can't get Rae to give me the recipe." Her eyes were so blue, Logan thought they had to be fake. Her hair color certainly was, though Logan hadn't seen a dark root in all the time he'd known her. He scanned her curvy body and wondered what was real and what wasn't.

Logan saw Tucker coming, and he ducked his head as if the other cowboy wouldn't see him. He had to get away before Tucker saw him talking to Layla, but his brain had taken a serious vacation.

Thankfully, a ripple went through the crowd, causing both Layla and Logan to turn. He thought perhaps Rae had come out in her wedding dress, but no. It was simply a car that had pulled up to the circle drive. Then Logan saw Sam.

He practically pushed aside wedding guests to get to the sidewalk. He half-jogged, half-walked to his brother, where he embraced him. "You made it."

"It's been rough." Sam clapped Logan on the back and stepped back. He drew Bonnie to his side, and Logan hugged her too.

"How's Boyfriend?"

"You didn't even ask me about my dog," Sam said.

Bonnie laughed. "Boyfriend is fine. He gets along great with Girlfriend."

"I guess that's what you want, right?" Logan stepped with them as they moved toward the wedding party. "I mean, I don't have a girlfriend, but if I did, I'd want to get along with her." He mentally commanded himself to stop talking. He cut a glance in Layla's direction and caught her watching him.

Or them. Maybe she was glad to see Bonnie again. Logan looked away. "I'll go tell Ben you're here." He strode toward the supply shed, his face hotter than the temperature called for. He wiped the sweat from under his hatband and determined not to look for Layla once he returned to the wedding.

———

Her Mistletoe Cowboy **is available now!** Order it in ebook, paperback, or audiobook by scanning the QR code below.

Her Billionaire Cowboy (Book 1): Tucker Jenkins has had enough of tall buildings, traffic, and has traded in his technology firm in New York City for Steeple Ridge Horse Farm in rural Vermont. Missy Marino has worked at the farm since she was a teen, and she's always dreamed of owning it. But her ex-husband left her with a truckload of debt, making her fantasies of owning the farm unfulfilled. Tucker didn't come to the country to find a new wife, but he supposes a woman could help him start over in Steeple Ridge. Will Tucker and Missy be able to navigate the shaky ground between them to find a new beginning?

Her Restless Cowboy: A Butters Brothers Novel, Steeple Ridge Romance (Book 2): Ben Buttars is the youngest of the four Buttars brothers who come to Steeple Ridge Farm, and he finally feels like he's landed somewhere he can make a life for himself. Reagan Cantwell is a decade older than Ben and the recreational direction for the town of Island Park. Though Ben is young, he knows what he wants—and that's Rae. Can she figure out how to put what matters most in her life—family and faith—above her job before she loses Ben?

Her Faithful Cowboy: A Butters Brothers Novel, Steeple Ridge Romance (Book 3): Sam Buttars has spent the last decade making sure he and his brothers stay together. They've been at Steeple Ridge for a while now, but with the youngest married and happy, the siren's call to return to his parents' farm in Wyoming is loud in Sam's ears. He'd just go if it weren't for beautiful Bonnie Sherman, who roped his heart the first time he saw her. Do Sam and Bonnie have the faith to find comfort in each other instead of in the people who've already passed?

Her Mistletoe Cowboy: A Butters Brothers Novel, Steeple Ridge Romance (Book 4): Logan Buttars has always been good-natured and happy-go-lucky. After watching two of his brothers settle down, he recognizes a void in his life he didn't know about. Veterinarian Layla Guyman has appreciated Logan's friendship and easy way with animals when he comes into the clinic to get the service dogs. But with his future at Steeple Ridge in the balance, she's not sure a relationship with him is worth the risk. Can she rely on her faith and employ patience to tame Logan's wild heart?

Her Patient Cowboy: A Butters Brothers Novel, Steeple Ridge Romance (Book 5): Darren Buttars is cool, collected, and quiet—and utterly devastated when his girlfriend of nine months, Farrah Irvine, breaks up with him because he wanted her to ride her horse in a parade. But Farrah doesn't ride anymore, a fact she made very clear to Darren. She returned to her childhood home with so much baggage, she doesn't know where to start with the unpacking. Darren's the only Buttars brother who isn't married, and he wants to make Island Park his permanent home—with Farrah. Can they find their way through the heartache to achieve a happily-ever-after together?

Graham (Book 1): Graham Whittaker returns to Coral Canyon a few days after Christmas—after the death of his father. He takes over the energy company his dad built from the ground up and buys a high-end lodge to live in—only a mile from the home of his once-best friend, Laney McAllister. They were best friends once, but Laney's always entertained feelings for him, and spending so much time with him while they make Christmas memories puts her heart in danger of getting broken again…

Eli (Book 2): Since the death of his wife a few years ago, Eli Whittaker has been running from one job to another, unable to find somewhere for him and his son to settle. Meg Palmer is Stockton's nanny, and she comes with her boss, Eli, to the lodge, her long-time crush on the man no different in Wyoming than it was on the beach. When she confesses her feelings for him and gets nothing in return, she's crushed, embarrassed, and unsure if she can stay in Coral Canyon for Christmas. Then Eli starts to show some feelings for her too…

Andrew (Book 3): Andrew Whittaker is the public face for the Whittaker Brothers' family energy company, and with his older brother's robot about to be announced, he needs a press secretary to help him get everything ready and tour the state to make the announcements. When he's hit by a protest sign being carried by the company's biggest opponent, Rebecca Collings, he learns with a few clicks that she has the background they need. He offers her the job of press secretary when she thought she was going to be arrested, and not only because the spark between them in so hot Andrew can't see straight.

Can Becca and Andrew work together and keep their relationship a secret? Or will hearts break in this classic romance retelling reminiscent of *Two Weeks Notice*?

Beau (Book 4): Beau Whittaker has watched his brothers find love one by one, but every attempt he's made has ended in disaster. Lily Everett has been in the spotlight since childhood and has half a dozen platinum records with her two sisters. She's taking a break from the brutal music industry and hiding out in Wyoming while her ex-husband continues to cause trouble for her. When she hears of Beau Whittaker and what he offers his clients, she wants to meet him. Beau is instantly attracted to Lily, but he tried a relationship with his last client that left a scar that still hasn't healed…

Can Lily use the spirit of Christmas to discover what matters most? Will Beau open his heart to the possibility of love with someone so different from him?

Todd (Book 5): Todd Christopherson has just retired from the professional rodeo circuit and returned to his hometown of Coral Canyon. Problem is, he's got no family there anymore, no land, and no job. Not that he needs a job--he's got plenty of money from his illustrious career riding bulls.

Then Todd gets thrown during a routine horseback ride up the canyon, and his only support as he recovers physically is the beautiful Violet Everett. She's no nurse, but she does the best she can for the handsome cowboy. **Will she lose her heart to the billionaire bull rider? Can Todd trust that God led him to Coral Canyon...and Vi?**

Liam (Book 6): Rose Everett isn't sure what to do with her life now that her country music career is on hold. After all, with both of her sisters in Coral Canyon, and one about to have a baby, they're not making albums anymore.

Liam Murphy has been working for Doctors Without Borders, but he's back in the US now, and looking to start a new clinic in Coral Canyon, where he spent his summers.

When Rose wins a date with Liam in a bachelor auction, their relationship blooms and grows quickly. **Can Liam and Rose find a solution to their problems that doesn't involve one of them leaving Coral Canyon with a broken heart?**

Finn (Book 7): Her sons want her to be happy, but she's too old to be set up on a blind date...isn't she?

Amanda Whittaker has been looking for a second chance at love since the death of her husband several years ago. Finley Barber is a cowboy in every sense of the word. Born and raised on a racehorse farm in Kentucky, he's since moved to Dog Valley and started his own breeding stable for champion horses. He hasn't dated in years, and everything about Amanda makes him nervous.

Will Amanda take the leap of faith required to be with Finn? Or will he become just another boyfriend who doesn't make the cut?

Zach (Book 8): When Celia Abbott-Armstrong runs into a gorgeous cowboy at her best friend's wedding, she decides she's ready to start dating again.

But the cowboy is Zach Zuckerman, and the Zuckermans and Abbotts have been at war for generations.

Can Zach and Celia find a way to reconcile their family's differences so they can have a future together?

Colton (Book 1): All the maid at Whiskey Mountain Lodge wants for her birthday is a handsome cowboy billionaire. And Colton can make that wish come true—if only he hadn't escaped to Coral Canyon after being left at the altar...

Wes (Book 2): She broke up with him to date another man...who broke her heart. He's a former CEO with nothing to do who can't get her out of his head. Can Wes and Bree find a way toward happily-ever-after at Whiskey Mountain Lodge?

Gray (Book 3): She's best friends with the single dad cowboy's brother and has watched two friends find love with the sexy new cowboys in town. When Gray Hammond comes to Whiskey Mountain Lodge with his son, will Elise finally get her own happily-ever-after with one of the Hammond brothers?

Cy (Book 4): A cowboy billionaire beast, his new manager, and the Christmas traditions that soften his heart and bring them together.

Ames (Book 5): A cowboy billionaire cop who's a stickler for rules, the woman he pulls over when he's not even on duty, and the personal mandates he has to break to keep her in his life...

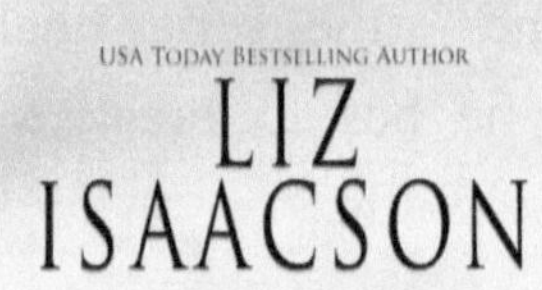

Rhett (Book 1): To save her business, she'll have to risk her heart. She needs a husband to be credible as a matchmaker. He wants to help a neighbor. **Will their fake marriage take them out of the friend zone?**

Tripp (Book 2): She needs a husband to keep her son. He's wanted to take their relationship to the next level, but she's always pushing him away. Will their trivial tie take them all the way to happily-ever-after?

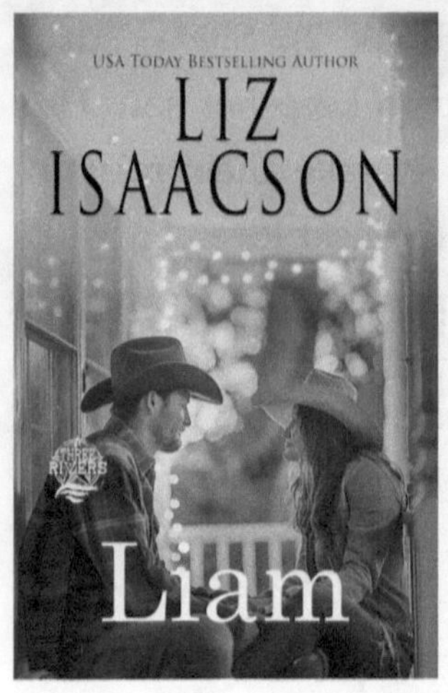

Liam (Book 3): She's desperate to save her ranch. He wants to help her any way he can. Will their invented I-Do open doors that have previously been closed and lead to a happily-ever-after for both of them?

Jeremiah (Book 4): He wants to prove to his brothers that he's not broken. She just wants him. Will a fake marriage heal him or push her further away?

Wyatt (Book 5): To get her inheritance, she needs a husband. He's wanted to fly with her for ages. Can their pretend pledge turn into something real?

Skyler (Book 6): She needs a new last name to stay in school. He's willing to help a fellow student. Can this wanna-be wife show the playboy that some things should be taken seriously?

Micah (Book 7): They were just actors auditioning for a play. The marriage was just for the audition – until a clerical error results in a legal marriage. Can these two ex-lovers negotiate this new ground between them and achieve new roles in each other's lives?

Gideon (Book 8): It's 1971, and Gideon Walker is on the cutting edge of all the technology coming out of Texas. He has big dreams and wants to make something of himself. Then he meets Penny Aarons, and everything changes. He only has eyes for her, but she's got plans and dreams of her own...

Read this origin romance for Momma and Daddy from the Seven Sons series today!

ABOUT LIZ

Liz Isaacson writes inspirational romance, usually set in Texas, or Wyoming, or anywhere else horses and cowboys exist. She lives in Utah, where she writes full-time, takes her two dogs to the park everyday, and eats a lot of veggies while writing. Find her on her website at feelgoodfictionbooks.com